KIERA'S C

Kristy Brown

For Darrell, Joseph and Jamie. xxx

AWAKENINGS

Chapter One

Zakk's throat grew tighter. Barely able to breathe, sweat dripped from his brow.

"What...what did I do wrong?" He gasped, seeing only darkness. Invisible hands clamped around his neck. "Please... stop." His limbs became heavy like lead weights. Knowing this to be the end, he managed to push out with a shallow breath, "I'm sorry."

The vice around his throat loosened, discarding him like a crumpled tissue. Maybe an apology was all 'it' needed. Minutes passed, feeling like an eternity. All seemed quiet in the icy air. Zakk dare not move. Trying to collect his thoughts, attempting to regulate his breathing. Straining to catch a glimpse of his jailer but was unable to see past his own shadow. The presence watched, enjoying the show. Waves of emotions passed within; pain, loneliness, emptiness, dread, but most of all fear. Fear seeping in, like black ink coursing through every vein, devouring all consciousness. For the first time ever, Zakk felt totally alone. He knew if he could scream, no one would hear. If he tried to run, his legs would not aid him.

"Who are you?"

"Who am I? Who am I?" The voice somehow seemed strangely familiar, as it broke into a spine-chilling laughter.

"Don't you know?" it mocked. "Look hard, deep into yourself. You know who I am. I am your darkest fear when you close your eyes. I lie in wait at your very core. Who am I?"

Zakk fiddled with the dull glass ring on his middle finger. It had belonged to his mother, just touching it reminded him of her warm smile, her golden silky hair, and the lullaby she sang to tuck him up each night.

"You're the Witch Queen!" he realised. He'd waited so long for answers but still was not face-to-face with this cold-blooded murderer. "You killed my mother."

"Clever, clever Zakky. Clever child," she hissed. "Your mother would be so proud of you."

Silence fell upon him. Aching with sadness, skin burning in anger. If he was about to die in this cave, he needed answers.

"Why her?"

"I should have ruled this world. I should have been queen. She was useless. I'll do better. It should have been me at your father's side. She never loved him." Spitting out the words as if they were poison.

"But you did?" Zakk asked. "You loved my father?"

"Silly boy, silly little, Zakky. I do not love. It's a weakness which eats you alive, swallows you whole then moves on to dessert." Had she tasted this bitter pain? "I got sweet revenge on sad, cowardly Helen by pushing her into a D'rog pit. They tore into her like a yummy treat."

Tears pushed under his eyelids. Unable to swallow, for the boulder-like lump blocking his windpipe.

"Tossed from one to the other, like a little raggedy doll," she sang, with great malice.

Zakk, now broken, wept. No longer able to hold the tears at bay. Giving in to the despair, picturing his mother's gruesome death. The Witch Queen poked a spindly leather finger into Zakk's cheek. Her face still covered by a veil of darkness. Watching his tears run down her long, ugly finger, he noticed a very familiar glass ring at the end of it. Shaking in disbelief, he looked again, recognising his father's ring. Time slowed. Sweat gushed over him like hot rain.

"Father!" he cried. "Father?" knowing the only response would be that of his own echoes chasing each other around the stone cave walls.

"He's gone," she said, stepping a little closer, he could just make out a pair of empty eyes. Searching them wildly for a hint of compassion, but there was none to be found. Like hard coal, these eyes were dead inside.

"No, no," he pleaded, kneeling on the floor, arms clasping his chest.

"I will rule Zantar; it is meant to be. All will live in fear of my gaze upon them. I thought you might have been my biggest barrier. But as I look upon you, crying like an infant, I find you weak, boy. It will be easy to send you to join your parents. It's only fair after all."

The Witch Queen took a step back; he could see her boney outline as she held her hands aloft and chanted. Flames shot from her hands and bolted toward him. Vibrant reds and dancing oranges licked at his heels, engulfing him, he stumbled back. The chanting became more urgent. Zakk raised both hands to shield his eyes. *This is it. I am finished. I couldn't save my family, or my people. I am nothing.*

At that moment, the air cooled. Opening an eye, feeling safe from the heat. A pure force of light shielded him, bringing the fire to a halt. Bizarrely, the force poured out from his mother's ring, which now shone all the colours of the rainbow. In her own way, she still watched over him and protected him. Feeling the wrath of the Witch Queen sliding away. Strength glided back through his being once more. Slowly rising to his feet, feeling strangely confident. This new resolve seemed to anger the witch further. She tried once again to execute her enemy, throwing arrow upon arrow of flesh stripping fire, but to no avail. Her efforts bounced off the protective shield, like hail against a windowpane.

"Damn your wretched mother and your proud father. If I cannot kill you, I'll make you wish I had."

A high-pitched squeal, a flash of white light, and Zakk began to fall. Unable to feel his body or open his eyes. There were no sounds. The heartbeat pounding in his chest moments ago, fell deathly silent, and all went black.

Chapter Two

Kiera cranked up the volume to the edge of its limits and danced around the room. Singing along, hairbrush in hand, throwing in the odd harmony or two. Imagining herself on a smoke-filled set, a wind machine blowing her hair wildly about her face for dramatic effect. She would be wearing a black off-the-shoulder number, combat trousers and army boots. Her almond eyes, dripping in eyeliner, her lips redder than anger itself. In reality, her chocolate brown hair was an uncombed mess pulled into a scrunchie atop her head, and she wore a green velvety dressing gown and Scooby-Doo slippers. Singing and twirling into the arms of an imaginary chiselled hunk, whilst strutting along the landing.

Kiera froze mid- breath. Maddy stood at the foot of the stairway, chewing her red frizzy hair, to stifle the laughter. "Your uncle let me in."

"How long have you been there?" Kiera asked, feeling herself blush from scrunchie to slippers.

"Long enough," Maddy teased. "Who'd have thought it? Kiera Matthews…by day, innocent schoolgirl, by night, secret diva!"

"Don't tell anyone," Kiera pleaded.

"Okay, okay, but you owe me an ice cream." Maddy smirked. "Came to see if you wanna go out? Thought we'd meet up with the boys at the beach."

"Cool," Kiera replied. "But give me chance to freshen up. Don't wanna scare 'em." She began attacking her hair with the brush.

Uncle Tom popped his head around the corner. "Will you be a doll and take Terrence? He's still settling in. Just watch him while I'm at work." Grinning at the girls, shoving the terrier onto Kiera. "Cheers!" he yelled, rushing out the door.

"Come on, you mangy mutt," Kiera rubbed his head. "Let's get your lead." Terrence bounded after her like a crazed monkey awaiting a banana.

"Err mate…you might wanna get dressed first!" Maddy shouted.

It was a beautiful, lazy day in the small seaside town of Stanforth. Being a week before tourist season, it was just the locals. Kiera had lived here with her uncle for as long as she could remember. She knew about her mother, some semi-famous country singer named Lynne Matthews. Her father's details were a little hazier. Apparently, he was a roadie. Kiera would receive the odd allowance cheque from her mother, but Uncle Tom dealt with all that. Lynne Matthews had gone on tour in Australia years ago and never returned. Kiera couldn't remember the woman and had become an expert at pretending not to care. Sometimes getting an overpowering urge to secretly Google the singer, but black and white facts about your birth mother just frustrated and angered her further. Photographs on-line of a smiling liar, made Kiera feel sick. If the subject of her parents ever arose, she would simply shrug off the sickly cramping knot in her gut. The pain of knowing that they didn't want her.

"Hey! Here comes speedy and weedy," shouted Daz, as he and Joe watched the girls rolling up. Kiera frowned; he always called them this, even though they were quite proficient on skates. They never questioned which was which, but both secretly hoped they were not the latter.

"What's this?" Joe asked. "Thought you were working in your uncle's shop today? You kill him off or something?"

"Whatever," Kiera shrugged. "I told you before, it pays for my singing lessons."

"His way of keeping tabs on you more like," Daz mumbled.

"He's in a good mood and the shops not busy yet," Kiera said, flicking Daz an evil look. "I do have to do the stock count tomorrow. Will you guys meet me afterward? There's a new Channing Tatum movie I wanna see."

"Oh, I do *soooo* love a Tatum." Joe raised an eyebrow.

"Me too, he's just so cute," Daz gushed.

The girls took off skating along the beach path. Maddy pulled Kiera's arm and they hung back from the boys.

"Notice how Joe's face lit up when he saw you?"

"No," Kiera replied, taking no nonsense of this 'Joe' rubbish. "We're just great friends, as I keep telling you."

"Well you just keep your blinkers on, missy," said Maddy, shaking her head. "That's what we think."

"We?" Kiera asked, coming to a halt.

"Me and Daz, we think you're made for each other." Maddy poked Kiera's side.

"You wanna know what I think? I think you two have got far too much time on your hands. Just because you and Daz are like, 'picking out curtains,' I'm here to tell you, there will be no joint wedding." Sticking her nose dramatically in the air, Kiera skated after Terrence.

The four friends hung out all day. The girls skated up and down, trying to impress the boys with their mediocre tricks. The boys pretended to ignore them, deep in conversation about the big sci-fi sequel due out, and Joe's new trial bike. The four seemed unbreakable. This was Kiera's family now. With them she felt wanted, happy, but if she stopped to think, for just a second, she became restless. Somewhere deep down inside, was a puzzle she couldn't solve. This feeling made her uneasy, so she buried it away and kept it hidden. In her dreams though, came the desire to seek it out. In her dreams something, or someone, was seeking her.

Chapter Three

"Eight Moshi Monsters, eleven Star Wars figures, thirty-two sets of marbles, nineteen buckets and spades," sang Kiera, to the tune of "A Partridge in a Pear Tree." Humming along, trying to keep a merry outlook on the monotonous task at hand. "Seven Whoopi cushions, eight kite sets, four packs of cards, and a weird looking, male- Barbie doll." She stopped singing and looked at the last item again. "You're not on my list. Must be a new promo line. I'll pop you on the desk, not sure what to do with you..." Kiera began counting again. "Twenty-one yo-yo's, nine skittle sets," she boomed in full soprano style.

Zakk's eyes shot open. He'd woken abruptly, startled, letting out an overwhelming gasp, as if he'd been held under water for centuries. A noise, a voice, greeted him like a chorus of birdsong. No, an angel, or some higher being. Was he dead then? Was this the afterlife? Unable to move. Strapped down, pinned by his arms and legs, and across his chest was a restricting band. Was this a coffin? There was no air. Panicking, his eyes darted about. Beginning to focus, seeing blurred outlines in various shades of grey.

Kiera wrote the last number on the worksheet and gazed at the clock. It was only five forty-five. *What shall I do till six?* Turning to file the day's findings, gaze falling upon the doll she'd put to one side.

"Oh yes, I forgot about you." Scanning the contents of the box. "Doll, clothes, shoes, ooh, and a cool ring…" Reaching down inside the box to try it on, her uncle wouldn't mind. Sliding a hand past the doll, she retrieved the ring. "Cool, it fits." Kiera had never seen one like it, simple in its design, yet quite unique. Its clear glass was cut into tiny squares, as she angled it differently, it threw out various reflective patterns. A prism of colours emanating a rainbow around the dimly lit storeroom. "Wow," she gasped.

"Help," Zakk whispered. *"Help."* There was no power in his voice. *"Anybody?"*

Kiera shuddered, like someone had walked over her grave.

"Please, help me." The voice was weak but audible. Kiera spun around. Shaking her head, laughing at herself. She wasn't usually in the shop alone, but Uncle Tom said as it was just a stock take and the store would be locked, it would be safe.

"God, I'm bored. Guess there's time to dress you, little prince. Or I could leave you in your royal underwear. I'll make you all handsome and put you in the window display. Who knows someone might buy you? So, now I'm talking to myself? Great." Kiera yanked the doll from the box, ripping it from the plastic binds.

Oh God, thought Zakk, as a giant hand came toward him. I'm not dead. I've shrunk! Closing his eyes, as a huge sun shone down, its brightness almost blinding.

Kiera adjusted the desk lamp over the doll, to see what went where. For a second, she could have sworn she caught the tiniest movement in the doll's eyes. *Must have been the ring catching the light or something…*she told herself, bringing the doll up toward her face for closer inspection.

Aaahh! this is it; a giant is going to eat me—alive! Trying to kick his way to freedom but still had no feeling in both legs. Paralysed. To be chewed alive… I should've asked for death when the witch offered it.

"Please don't eat me," Zakk begged. "Do it quickly, don't chew, quick!"

Kiera gasped, hurling the doll to the far side of the room. "No way! No way! Did you just speak?" Backing up into the corner.

Zakk tornadoed through space, hitting the wall on the other side of the room, sprawling like wet spaghetti onto the floor.

Knock knock. Kiera jumped then remembered the guys would be

waiting at the front of the store. Running up the basement stairs and through the shop, she fumbled about with the huge bunch of keys, "Come on…come on!" Eventually unlocking the door, Kiera fled from the building, leaving the little doll half-dressed inside.

"What's up? You look like you've seen a ghost." Joe asked, when she nearly tripped over his feet.

"Come on, get a move on, we've been here at least a minute!" Daz laughed. Kiera ripped the ring from her finger and stuffed it into her jeans pocket. Composing herself, before turning to join her friends.

Zakk's terror grew stronger now than his earlier encounter with evil itself. A clown and a plastic dinosaur towered above. Were they guarding him until the strange giant returned? Or were they here to torture him? Was this the Witch Queen's idea of fun? He had so many questions. He lay motionless. What in the name of Zantar was happening? Unable to connect with his destiny, all consciousness faded, he became lost once more.

"Come on, we'll be late. We can't keep Channing waiting!" Maddy linked arms with Kiera, dragging her along. Kiera glanced back toward the shop. Alarm bells rang frantically within, her pulse pounding in her ears. *What on Earth just happened?*

Chapter Four

The circular shaped room had prison bars instead of walls like a giant birdcage, only there were no beautiful birds chirping away inside. Dozens of prisoners were held by the bars and looked in toward the Witch Queen on her throne—the vulture of death. The room was sparse of objects and atmosphere and reeked of betrayal and stale meat.

"You sshould pull the curtainsss acrosss, My Queen," hissed Googe, the Witch Queen's loyal imp. "You sshould not have to look upon ssuch plague."

The queen was vaguely bemused, as Googe had obviously never seen his own lizard-like reflection.

"I'm feeling down today, Googey, and it cheers me to see their misery."

"Yesss, Your Majesssty, asss you wisssh," whistled Googe through his snake-like tongue.

"Who's next on the list? The pit's becoming restless. Feed it, I'm sick of its constant moaning." The Witch Queen marched over to the surrounding cell, letting her gaze rove among the many possible victims. Dragging her long, spindly fingers across the bars, making a 'chinking' sound with the stolen ring.

The prisoners scurried backward, hoping to avoid her death penalty stare.

"You!" she pointed at a poor, petrified subject. "Get that one; he's nice and plump, should fill a hole nicely."

Googe unlocked the cell door and frog-marched the man to the mouth of the pit.

"Please," the prisoner begged. "I have a family. How will they feed themselves? Show mercy."

"Shut up! You imbecile. How dare you speak to your Queen! Do it," she commanded.

Googe gave him an almighty shove, as the man was almost twice his size. He fell without noise, as if the air itself held its breath. The moaning from the pit altered to a dull murmur.

"Next," she yelled.

A silhouette darkened the doorway.

"Ah, you! I've been waiting days for you. What news do you bring?"

"I have no news, My Queen," replied the visitor.

"What? You've had years to find the girl, and you haven't whittled it down at all?" Nostrils flaring. Fists clenching, sinking her nails into her palms. "I may as well kill you now and not waste any more precious time!"

The visitor gulped. "Oh no, Majesty. I've narrowed it down. She's definitely living in Stanforth."

The queen spun on her heels. "I know that, you moron! Googe, the pit sounds hungry again, feed it, will you."

Googe manhandled the visitor to the edge of the famously feared pit. They both looked down into it. It was foretold that at its belly were thousands of restless souls lost in nightmares, always waiting to awake but never would.

"Wait! I've narrowed it down to three," the visitor's voice trembled.

"Stop, Googe." She paused. "Bring the fool here." Her face changing slowly, into a false friendliness. "Well that's more like it," she muttered through a clenched smile.

"I've looked for the signs, like you said. You know, a regal beauty, voice sweeter than a Hyug's kiss, melts over you like honey..."

"Go on." Her eyes narrowed upon the informant's lips.

"Lucky for us, there's a talent competition at school Friday night."

"It hardly gives us much time," she spat.

"The three girls are all entered, so she will give herself away."

"Excellent idea. And what of the ring?" The Witch Queen unclenched.

"No sign, Your Highness," the visitor replied, staring at the ground.

"Well find it! Whoever has it will lead us to a certain prince. Two birds, one stone. Get it, idiot?" she snapped, adjusting the over-sized stolen crown.

"Yes, Majesty, I will get on it right away." The visitor sped toward the exit.

"Oh, and by the way," she added. "It's Prince Zakky's birthday on Friday too, which only leaves five days."

The visitor halted. "What happens then?"

"Yesss," added Googe, looking slightly baffled. "Do tell usss, Majesssty."

"If she doesn't have both rings in her possession by Zakk's sixteenth, he will be plastic forever, leaving me outright ruler, and total power will at last be mine," she bellowed, with a touch of insanity. "Brilliant, eh? I may not have had the power to kill him, but I've left the boy in ultimate torment."

"But, Your Majesty," the visitor dared to ask. "Why bother? I mean, the girl probably doesn't even know anything. There are no signs."

"The prophecy will be fulfilled. I 've seen it in my visions. Only the ending will be different...She will die. I want her gone, just in case. There is no room for error. The girl, the ring, or the prince will save your

18

life for now. A hat trick, and you will be set free. You have five days!"
Raising a crooked brow, she waved the visitor away.

"Googe, show our guest out."

"What about my—"

"Be silent, such matters don't concern you right now. Leave this instant."

Five days, five days! The visitor panicked. Tension shooting through their body like bullets. *In five days, my life will surely end.* The visitor raced past the castle walls and stood before the vortex, for possibly the last time.

"No matter what, I have to get that ring. We have to be free."

"Nooohhh," screamed Zakk and Kiera simultaneously. Both bolted upright, sweating, relieved that it was just another awful nightmare. Feeling awkward that someone else was sharing their dreams. They'd felt like this for a while, but lately it had become more intense. Their privacy had been invaded, like someone was watching the gig without a ticket. For years now, Kiera dreamt of breathtaking landscapes in soft, inviting pastels, silver streams trickling to a chorus of hypnotic birdsong. Upon turning thirteen, her nights were filled with flashes of contorted faces, people's screams, hints of an evil shadow beckoning. Amazing landscapes and quirky creatures that surely could not exist. The images were now in Technicolor; it was becoming harder each night to stay out of the cold, suffocating darkness. Zakk had heard music and seen gadgets that made no sense. People dressed in strange clothing. Transport that should not exist. Both tried to put it down to having vivid imaginations, but this had been the first time they felt a definite presence.

Zakk looked around remembering his predicament. The silent guards were still watching over him. Still in his underwear, he lay shivering. Tingles shot up and down his plastic frame. At last, able to feel sensation in his arms and legs but couldn't move them.

Kiera rushed down to breakfast. School was beckoning; it might take her mind off the bizarre goings-on lately.

"Morning, sleepy head."

"Morning," she groaned back at her uncle with one eye half closed.

"Hey, isn't it your big singing debut this Friday?"

"Guess so." She shrugged.

"Want me to come? What are you singing? Are you nervous?"

Kiera wasn't in the mood for twenty questions.

"Up to you, haven't decided, and very," she snapped, grabbing a piece of toast. "I've gotta go. I'll be late."

Tom grabbed his niece's arm. "Kiera, is everything all right?"

"Yes," she replied, unable to keep eye contact. "Why do you ask?"

"No reason, you just seem a little distant, that's all."

"Oh, it must be competition jitters." Pausing for a second, "Uncle Tom, I-I."

"Yes?" Looking over his glasses.

She desperately wanted to share with him these strange events. And not just what happened yesterday at the store. She wanted to tell him everything about these feelings she'd always had, that she didn't belong, that she was different. Feeling that someone was always watching her. The sense of being almost awake in her sleep, that something was sharing her dreams. So many questions flooded her thoughts, unsure if Tom would be able to answer them. *If I mention the talking doll… will he think I'm crazy? Once you say it out loud, there's no taking it back…*

"Oh nothing, I've forgotten what I was going to say. Silly me." She kissed him on the cheek, grabbed her rucksack, and made for the door.

* * * *

Kiera counted the last minutes down on her watch. The day had been long; she'd felt anxiously restless. Finally, the school bell rang. *Home time at last!* The whole day had been spent glaring out of various windows. Feeling uneasy; unease loomed over her like a bad smell.

"Before everyone leaves, Kiera Matthews, would you like to give us the answer?" Miss Ing squeaked.

"Err, dunno, Miss. Sorry," Kiera replied, continuing to stare into the distance.

"You may all go. Kiera, may I have a quick word?" asked the concerned looking teacher.

"I'll wait for you in the corridor," Joe informed her, as the pupils filed past.

"Is there a problem, Kiera?"

"No, Miss." Kiera shrugged.

"Well, it's just that you haven't been your normal studious self today. Is there anything I can help you with?"

"No, Miss." Inching toward the door.

"Well, my door's always open."

"Yes, Miss, thanks, Miss, bye." Kiera escaped, musing that if Miss Ing were any more mouse-ish, she'd grow whiskers. Out in the corridor, she grabbed Joe's arm and marched him out the school entrance. "God, that woman really lives up to her name, she definitely is a bit *missing*!" Kiera walked quickly, glancing down at her watch. "Everyone's allowed an off day, but oh no, not Kiera. Not good old reliable Kiera."

"Kiera, there's something I want to talk to you about," Joe said, galloping alongside to Madam Swift's house for her singing lesson.

"Hmmm?" Kiera murmured uninterested. In her head, thoughts of voices, dreams and dolls, spun like a launderette on a Sunday.

"Yes," he continued. "I wanted to ask you if—"

"Spit it out, Joe! I haven't got time to guess," Kiera snapped.

"What's with you? No need to bite my head off. Miss Ing might be squeaky and annoying, but she's right, you're not yourself today." Joe flounced away, leaving her feeling rather foolish.

* * * *

"Come on, Miss Matthews, you can do better than that. Try it again, and this time give it a little more oomph!" ordered the robust music teacher. She wasn't the most feminine of women, towering over most men; almost 'fridge-like' in size. Her warm breath smelt like teabags and toast. Kiera couldn't help focusing on her Chaplin-like moustache whenever she spoke.

She began to sing "Somewhere over the Rainbow."

"It's better," boomed Madam Swift in a low, monotone voice. "But your heart just doesn't seem in it today. Have you chosen a song for Friday's contest yet?"

"It's either this one, 'Memories,' or 'Shake It Off;' you know, something a bit funkier, and up-beat." Kiera flashed a dazzling smile. Madam Swift looked unimpressed. "It's by Taylor Swift," Kiera said.

"Yes, Miss Matthews, I am aware of her work. I just don't think it will do your voice justice."

* * * *

Six o'clock. Kiera left the lesson and started home. Deep in thought, and humming to herself, a hand grabbed her shoulder from behind. Kiera spun in horror.

"Oh my God, Joe! You scared the life out of me. What you doing here?"

"I wanted to say sorry for earlier and finish our talk."

"Oh no, Joe, it's me who's sorry. I was horrible. You know, time of the month or something," she blurted. Both stood in awkward silence, Joe a deep shade of crimson.

"Hey," Joe said, breaking the ice. "That tune you were humming was really catchy."

"Oh, was I humming?"

"So, what are you doing here? Didn't realize you were working tonight," Joe asked.

"Oh!" Kiera realised they were standing right outside the shop doorway.

"What on Earth?" she whispered. Kiera knew her head had given her feet direct instructions to go straight home. "Err, I've just got to collect something." It was time to face her fears and collect the doll, just to prove to herself that she wasn't going crazy. Either way, she had to know the truth. *It's now or never…*

"Hang on a minute, Kiera," Joe said, voice cracking. "I was wondering if you wanted to grab a pizza after the competition?"

"Sure, that'll be great," she said, grabbing the store keys from her rucksack.

"Really?" Joe grinned.

Oh pants… is he asking me out? Do I want that? I'm not ready for everything to change…what if we fall out, I can't lose him… Okay, be diplomatic.

"Yes, that'll be cool. The four of us celebrating my winning, or consoling my defeat," she joked. Joe looked deflated. Kiera didn't like hurting him, but right now, there was more pressing issues. "Wait here a sec. I won't be long."

Kiera escaped into the store and down into the basement. She stood over the doll in the stockroom. In her mind, daring it to speak, not knowing what her reaction would be if it did. She grabbed for it, shoving it in her rucksack.

"Ready," she told Joe whilst locking up. "Let's get out of here."

That night, Kiera sat up in bed, staring at the bag in the corner. The clock ticked on. One o'clock. A quarter to two. Twenty to three. Drilling her feet along the bed sheets, determined to stay awake. She had to know. Maybe she was just over-tired. There was lots of stuff on her mind: school tests, talent competition, work, and now Joe's feelings to contend with. Ten past three, and the bag hadn't moved.

This is silly! Her eyes gave in to the heaviness of night. In her dreams, she visited the place where she usually felt safe. But lately, Kiera found herself locked in this confusing, terrifying nightmare. Night after night, the same theme played out on loop. She was running; hunted by a 'thing' she couldn't quite see. The panting buzzed against her ear, its rancid breath, hot against her neck. Every night, it got a little closer, almost within touching distance. There was also another being in this vivid chase. A protector. Faceless and fearless, strong and determined. Kiera tried to focus on his face, the one who saved her from the monsters in her mind. Yet, his features were just a blur. Without this unknown saviour, Kiera would've never closed her eyes again.

Chapter Six

"Right, who is humming?" barked Mr. Thirtle, the tetchy science teacher. Kiera had come to think of him as a bothersome ferret. The students looked up from their test papers. "Well," he demanded. "I'm waiting."

The whole class shrugged, looking sheepishly amongst one another. "One more peep, and the person responsible shall fail and redo the test after school."

A few minutes passed, and Kiera felt eyes boring into her. Slowly, looking up and realising it was thirty pairs of eyes. Everyone seemed very interested in her.

"Kiera Matthews! Are you aware that you are humming?"

Kiera gulped. She had never really been told off before, apart from the time when she flicked a rubber band at Chloe Wilson's head, the girl was asking for it that day. But Kiera wasn't humming, was she?

"Well now, don't do it again. Last chance." Mr. Thirtle's voice softened. "Back to work all of you. Fifteen minutes remaining."

After yo-yoing, in and out of consciousness, Zakk awoke. He was somewhere different now, somewhere stuffy and claustrophobic. His face shoved against a pencil, and a giant hairbrush stuck into his back.

"Hello," Zakk moaned. "Hello, is anyone there?" Kicking out in frustration.

Kiera's head shot up, her pen fell to the floor, disturbing the silence yet again. She bent to retrieve it. On the way back up, she caught the narrowed eye of Mr. Thirtle. "Sorry," she mouthed.

What just happened? Then it dawned on her. That 'thing' was still in her rucksack and was now trying to rip its way to freedom. *Oh God. What's happening? Is this real?*

Zakk decided he'd had enough. This giant's hospitality was beyond belief. If death were to be his path, then he'd rather walk it, than live in this nightmare. He gave an almighty kick.

"Aaaww," Kiera yelped on being kicked in the back. Shooting up from the desk. Laughter broke out across the classroom.

"What do you think you're doing? Explain yourself, young lady!" Mr. Thirtle's face turned purple, his ferret nose twitched. Kiera flustered. Her skin burning from embarrassment. Grabbing the bag, she ran from the classroom, chased out by the thunderous laughter.

Running to the toilets, she locked herself in a cubicle and slumped to the ground crying. A few moments passed, and the well of tears dried up to a sniffle. A strange calmness swept over her. Feeling oddly at peace, like she hadn't done in years. She pulled the strange object from the bag that started all this, the doll. Holding it closer to study it. "Why am I not frightened? Because I'm crazy, that's why."

Zakk looked at the giant's heart-shaped face, taking in every inch of it. Looking into her almond eyes, he saw his own sadness reflected. Instantly feeling enormous empathy for this creature. He, too, was no longer afraid.

"Go on then," Kiera sniffled, breaking the silence. "Go on, I dare you! Speak. I know you can."

"Err, hello? And by the way, I'm not deaf." Zakk rubbed his plastic ears. "So, you're not going to eat me then?"

"Huh? What? Err, no…" Kiera screwed her face up. She had so many questions for this tiny being. "Who, what are you?"

"I am Zakk. This is not my world, is it?"

Kiera could hear tears hiding in his throat. "No, I'm afraid not. This is Earth. You are, well, you're a doll. Have you always been a doll? Cos if you have, I meant no offence."

"What? What are you talking about?" Zakk gasped.

"You're like plastic, a toy."

"Will you show me? I want to see."

Kiera got to her feet, unlocked the cubicle door, and held him up to the mirror. "That isn't me! What did she do to me? What in the name of Zantar is that?"

"Calm down, don't panic." Kiera hushed him.

"Don't panic. Don't panic! Are you mad? Firstly, I'm a *doll*. You are a giant. The Witch Queen's killed my parents and is probably ruling my world as we speak. I've failed my people. My dreams are so horrifying that I try not to sleep. I'm cold and alone. Nothing makes sense."

"I thought I had it bad," Kiera whispered. "Thought I was going crazy, but then you must be too. This is nuts. You need to go back to your world. I want everything back to normal. Is there anything I can do to help? To make all this go away?"

"If only you could… It's strange," he whispered. "I feel like I know you, like you've always been with me...somehow…"

"I feel the same," Kiera replied. "Like your voice, I've heard it before. I know it well. How…?"

Zakk searched Kiera's tear-stained face. Her cheeks still flushed. "We must have met before." He mused. "That's it," he roared. "We've met in our dreams. You're the girl…It is you, isn't it?"

"Yes," Kiera gasped. "You're the one helping me through the maze of nightmares. I've never seen your face, but it's you. What does this all mean?"

"I think," replied Zakk. "I think I have been sent to you for a reason. Shhhh!" Zakk stopped abruptly. Kiera held her breath. "I heard a noise," he whispered.

Kiera placed Zakk in-between the taps and went to investigate. "Now don't go falling in."

"Very funny," he said, crossing his doll arms.

"No, coast is clear." Kiera knelt at the sink, meeting with Zakk's eye level. "So, you can see and feel, but you're trapped in this plastic form?"

"Yes."

"Tell me the whole story. I'm in trouble now anyway." Kiera shrugged.

Zakk filled her in on the Witch Queen and his parents. Kiera gasped and shook her head throughout. He told her about the spell upon him—that if he weren't crowned by his sixteenth birthday, he would lose the right to rule. *Wow, a genuine prince.* Losing herself for a moment, imagining him down on one knee, begging her hand in marriage. *Queen Kiera!* She sighed deeply.

"Err, hello. Anybody there?" Zakk waved his hands past her eyes.

"Oh, sorry. Kinda phased out for a second there. I'm freaking out at the other realms and stuff…this is a lot for a girl to take in. Maybe it was easier to think I was crazy. So, how come?"

"How come what?"

"How come you're a doll?"

"Not sure," he shrugged. "The witch chanted something just before I blacked out. I think I'd be dead if it weren't for my mother's ring."

"How twisted. Talk about rubbing your face in it." Kiera mused.

"Rubbing my face in what?"

"You really are from a different world." Kiera laughed. "By the way, I'm Kiera." She grabbed his tiny hand and shook it. *This is so freaky.*

"I'm Zakk, Prince of Zantar. It's nice to meet you finally. Please tell me you still have the ring…"

"Here she is, Mrs. Jackson," Chloe Wilson yelled from the doorway. Her jet-black bob straightened to perfection, her apple-green eyes alight with triumph. "I told you Kiera was skipping class."

"This world will at last be mine." The Witch Queen's wrath dripped through the buttery sunset, like oil. Her dark poison blotted out the soft silvery skies above, as the life drained from Zantar's pulse. Thousands of fledglings slipped over the leaded skies, attempting to escape the emptiness. Destruction and chaos lashed from her fingertips, taking the soft pastel breath from a world once magnanimous of beauty. Now everything was stripped to bone and matter. The angry sea roared to her call like a humble servant, washing away memories of all that was once bright and alive.

"Yes, yes. I like it; it's glorious; it's so me," she howled.

"You have temporary ownership, yes. But time runs out. Others will come as it is foretold, and you will be nothing once again."

"Who dared to speak?" the Witch Queen asked in disbelief. Looking down at the king's 'so-called' army, kneeling on all fours under her invisible restraints. "Who dares? Who dares defy their queen?" Silence. "Nobody? Oh well, I'll just have to start killing you one by one until luck finds the right man." Flashing an evil yellow smile.

"It was I," called a disgruntled voice from behind.

"Oh." Walking slowly to the guard, her giraffe-like body clicking to the beat of her pointed boots. Bending low, grabbing his face. "How very brave and stupid of you. Well, well, if it isn't the king's lieutenant. Where is the captain I wonder? Can you tell me where he might be hiding?"

"He's not hiding; he's no coward. He's on a mission."

"Oh, but now I simply must know." Grabbing harder, sinking her tawny nails into his skin.

"I answer only to the king."

"Pity that. I don't think he'll be asking anything where he's gone."
She laughed, standing upright. "I'd just love to kill all of you. But that
would be such a waste. I have a much better plan for you, Lieutenant.
You and your band of 'merry little men.' Take them!"

The cave walls began to crack and rumble. Small rocks tumbled,
bouncing off the soldiers, and soon a mini avalanche threatened their
lives. A deafening ripping sound startled them, as monstrous shapes
began slowly forming into mountainous beings. One by one, they tore
away from the cave walls. A dozen giant, eyeless, stone monsters loomed
over the men. Lifting the soldiers above their boulder-shaped heads,
tossing them like marbles.

"Enough fun for now." The Witch Queen clapped. "Round 'em up
boys." The rock beings crunched slowly toward the cowering army. "At
last, things are finally looking up. I have the king's famous guards. Zantar
looks simply radiant under my new colour scheme. Out with the rainbow
vomit, in with the lifeless. This day just couldn't get any better, wouldn't
you agree, Googey?"

The little sidekick hissed and bowed as he led the king's troops to
the iron doors.

"You won't get away with this," shouted the lieutenant.

"Oh, but I think I just have. What the—?" The queen halted mid
breath. Cold dread clenched at her chest.

"My Queen. What'sss wrong?" asked Googe, scurrying to her side.

"We have a spectator, Googe." The Witch Queen shifted her focus.
"Don't just watch, my dear. Come, come join us."

Kiera froze. The Witch Queen's grey eyes burned into her mind.

Breathless, Kiera couldn't move. The stone-like eyes still scolded her mind. The words, 'come join us,' rang in her ears. The dreaded Witch Queen had seen her and now beckoned.

"Kiera? Are you all right?" Mrs. Jackson asked, placing a hand on Kiera's shoulder. Kiera pulled herself back into the room with a mighty gasp. "What's wrong, dear?"

"I-I'm not sure."

"Well," continued the egg-like Headmistress, "I cannot get any sense out of you. I'm calling for reinforcements." She smiled, picking up the phone. "Ms. Watson, could you step into my office please."

Oh brill, I so haven't got time to see the school counsellor. I must get back to Zakk; I'm all he's got. The bell rang for home time. *No! Not Yet!* Kiera's eyes darted to the clock on the wall.

"Miss Matthews, are you okay? You look a little pale." Mrs. Jackson asked.

"Err, no. I'm not." Kiera stood. "I'm not well at all. In fact, I think I need to go." Praying Mrs. Jackson wouldn't see through her best, sad puppy face. She had to reach Zakk before someone else did. The door opened as the meek counsellor entered.

"Ah, Ms. Watson, could you just have a little chat with, Kiera? She's not feeling herself today." She whispered the rest in her colleague's ear and left the room, giving Kiera a patronising smile. Kiera puffed her cheeks out and sat back down.

"Well now, how are we today?" Ms. Watson took a pew behind the overly tidy desk. Kiera thought Ms. Watson was the most approachable teacher here. She was pretty, in an understated way. If she put a little effort in, Ms. Watson could do a lot more with herself. Maybe apply a bit of make-up and leave her hair down for special occasions. And usually Kiera wouldn't mind chatting to her, but not today.

"Kiera, is there anything you want to share?" Silence. "How are you feeling now?" Silence. "You are not in trouble; we just want to understand why you left your lesson and didn't return?"

Kiera concentrated hard on her trainers, feet fighting each other; itching to get to Zakk.

"Whom were you speaking with in the toilet?" Ms. Watson asked softly. "Was there another girl missing class with you?" Silence. "You must tell me who she is."

"No, it wasn't a girl," Kiera blurted.

"So, it was a boy? What's his name? Whose class is he in? I'll have to have a chat with him; too, I'm afraid. We understand young love, feelings of the heart... Maybe next time you could meet this boy during break?"

"No, no, it's not like that at all..." Kiera whimpered, helplessly looking at the clock. "He's not a boy, he—" Stopping mid-flow. *Shut up you pratt*, her inner voice screamed.

"He's not a boy?" Ms. Watson seemed intrigued. A little too interested, for Kiera's liking.

"No, Miss, I was talking to myself." Kiera wished her focus had remained on her shoes. Ms. Watson frowned. She didn't seem to be buying any of it.

"So, now you're saying you were alone in the toilet?" Her eyes narrowed.

"Yes, Miss, I've got to go now, I feel sick." Putting a hand over her mouth and fleeing from the room. *Well, I made a total pig's ear of that.* She formula-one'd toward the girls' toilet.

Kiera zoomed around the doorway like a roller coaster on rails, coming to a sudden halt. The sink where Zakk had perched was overflowing.

"Oh my God, he's drowned!" Placing one foot in front of the other. Her body seemed to be stuck on pause. It was the longest short walk ever. She peered into the sink. "Thank God, he's not here." Relief quickly turned to horror. *Then, where is he? The Witch Queen must have taken him.* "It's all my fault." Written on the mirror above the sink, were the crimson lipstick words, 'I've got your little boyfriend, come and get him.'

Kiera's mind raced with terror, yet her gut told her Zakk was still alive. The urge to fight for him pushed her onward. Running toward the school exit, barging kids as she darted between them.

"Hey, watch it," Maddy yelled as she was knocked into a wall. "Kiera?"

"Sorry!" Kiera yelled absently.

* * * *

Kiera entered the playground. A large group of students huddled together. She joined them, as if some force was pulling her forward. Joe appeared at her side.

"Hey, are you okay? What's happening?" Kiera ignored the question, continuing to watch the action.

"Must be a fight," she said vacantly, drowned out by all the laughter and cheering. Maddy finally arrived.

"Well?" she asked, a little out of breath.

"No idea," Joe replied. "She's in a trance or something. It's weird."

"Should we call her uncle? He'd know what to do," Maddy whispered.

"Don't include him." Kiera snapped. "I'm not deaf you know."

"Sorry," Joe muttered. Through a gap in the crowd, Kiera spotted Chloe Wilson, one half of the evil duo. Was she fighting? Who with?

"Help me! Help me!" a little voice cried out above their heads. "Kiera, where are you? Help me!" It was Zakk, zigzagging above the crowd. Chloe and her horrible twin Ben were tossing him across the circle.

"Stop it, you idiots," Kiera screamed, pushing through the fog of hecklers.

"Catch it piggy, if you can," laughed Ben, throwing Zakk higher. The crowd of faces blurred into one long pair of lips, taunting and ridiculing her. Kiera jumped, pathetically waving both arms about.

"Kiera's into Barbies," a voice snarled.

"Can I be your Action Man?" and "Freak," were amongst the jeers.

"Give it back, Wilson," Joe demanded, snatching the doll, pushing Ben to the ground.

"Oh, here's your knight in shining armour," Ben shouted. Kiera, Joe and Maddy made for the school gates. "Oh, but you prefer dollies don't you, you saddo!"

"Keep walking, just ignore him," Joe instructed.

"Must kill you that she doesn't want you, Joey."

Joe spun, glaring at Ben. "Shut up, Wilson, or I'll deck you again."

"Whatever, Crosby," Ben smirked, dusting himself down, before walking away. The crowd dispersed; murmurs of Kiera's name hung in the air. Joe handed her the doll.

"What's going on with you?" Maddy asked sheepishly, eyeing the toy.

"I can't explain right now." Kiera wrapped Zakk in her scarf and placed him in her bag.

"Hey guys," shouted Daz, who was leaning against the school gates. Dressed in a black leather jacket, his black, spiky hair waxed to perfection. "What's the drama?"

"Look, I know you're all worried, but you wouldn't believe me if I told you," Kiera sighed.

"Try me," Joe urged, grabbing her elbow.

"I can't Joe, not this time." Looking into his worried eyes. "I'm okay, I'll be fine. Just need a bit of space." She walked away.

"What have I missed?" Daz kissed Maddy's cheek.

"Well…" She replied, taking a deep breath.

Kiera walked home quickly, leaving her friends behind in confusion.

"Are you okay?"

"Yes," replied Zakk. "Apart from a banging headache, and I seem to have lost the little clothing I had."

A few yards down the road Kiera stopped for a moment. A feeling of dread hounded her, like someone was stealing her footsteps.

"Joe!" She spun to face him, "Will you stop sneaking…" But the street was empty. "That's weird. Maybe I just need some sleep and possibly a reality check, but then, whose reality would I be checking?" she mused.

"Are you talking to me?" Zakk asked through the bag.

"If you like," she replied. "If you like."

Somebody held Kiera's hand. A familiar voice whispered in her ear. She smiled in her sleep and felt safe. Bliss soon turned to anguish.

"Run, Kiera, run! They're coming for us. Stay with me, keep up," Zakk *called, dragging her by the arm. "Where did you put the ring? It's our only hope." She turned slowly, focusing on a blurred vision of huge, black dog-like creatures, their fangs dripping with blood and slime.*

"We can stop them," a voice said. "But you must tell me where you put the ring!"

The voice altered from Zakk's deep soft tones, to a menacing hysterical scream. "Tell me, tell me," it commanded. "Where is it?"

"Kiera, wake up!" Zakk shouted. "Don't tell her, you must never tell her!"

A pair of cold-stone eyes pierced through her dream. Kiera awoke with a gasp. "Zakk, where are you?" She trembled.

"I'm right here," he said gently, perched on the pillow, as if to guard her. "It's okay, you were dreaming again."

"W-what were those creatures?"

"They are the D'rogs."

"D'rogs?" questioned Kiera. "What does the 'D' stand for?"

"Death. They killed my mother." A single tear rolled down his plastic face.

"Oh, Zakk, I'm so sorry." Kiera placed her finger over his tiny hand. "What's happening to me?"

"She's after you now. Finding your dreams and hiding in them," Zakk sighed.

"But you were with me. I felt you there."

"Yes, I was, but she's blurring me out. She's so powerful now."

"But I didn't tell her did I, Zakk? She doesn't know where the ring is?"

"No, don't worry," Zakk reassured. "If you had, she would be here with us now. Lay down and get some rest."

"How can she be in my dreams? I don't understand."

"Whilst she has my father's ring, the witch has the power to track your mind in its unconscious state. It must greatly frustrate her that she cannot find you."

Kiera closed her eyes, not knowing which reality she felt safer in.

"Trust no-one, except me," Zakk warned. "There are spies in many dimensions, especially this one now that she knows I'm here, and we are together. She feels the ring's power. The two rings are a marriage; they belong together."

"Too much information, my head may explode. I'm going to sleep now; I'm exhausted." Turning onto her side, away from his gaze. *I trust my Uncle Tom, and my friends,* she thought as she started to drift off.

"You will put them in danger if you tell them," Zakk said, guessing her thoughts.

"You can read my mind, too? This is too weird. Pack it in, you're freaking me out." Shoving the pillow over her head, Kiera tried to go back to sleep.

* * * *

"Damn, blast it," shouted the Witch Queen, throwing the goblet to the ground.

"What'sss wrong, Your Highnesss?" asked Googe, rushing in to attend to her.

"The prince is onto us. Keeping the girl one step ahead. Go find our 'friend' and insist that they hurry things along."

"But, Misstresss, I do not know where they dwell," Googe grimaced.

"How about the school, idiot! Take Albatron. He'll track them down. Before you go, clear up that mess," she ordered, pointing at the goblet of spilt wine. "And Googe, look after my baby, he hasn't had a good flight since that scuffle with that crazed pet beast of the former king."

"Yesss, Ma'am." Googe hesitated. "Are you ssure you want me to take Albatron? He doesss get a little vortex ssicknesss."

"Don't be absurd, my Alby is totally vortex approved. I trained him myself. Now go," she bellowed, nearly taking Googe off his over-sized feet.

* * * *

"Morning. Did you sleep a little better? Are you going to school today, Kiera?" Zakk asked, as she stared vacantly through her reflection in the mirror.

"Guess I have to," she yawned, "don't want Uncle Tom asking questions. He's so overprotective. Guess I've gotta face the music sometime. Pants, it's the school competition tomorrow night, so I can't be off."

"You could sing 'happy birthday' to me," Zakk joked. "Have you chosen a song yet? You could try out a few on me, if you like."

"Err, no thanks, I'd be too embarrassed. You'll laugh or think I'm rubbish."

"You're quite a complex girl, Kiera Matthews," Zakk chuckled. "Am I coming to school again today?"

"You sure you want to, after yesterday's nightmare?"

"I don't want to be seen in this garment, that's for sure!" Kiera had dressed him with an old pair of Barbie dungarees, which were itchy and pink.

"It's definitely your colour." She beamed. Zakk shook his head. "Sorry," she said, biting her lip. "Things can't get any worse, eh?"

"Oh, they can, and they will," He shuddered.

"I'll come straight home, Zakk, I promise. Take some time to think of our next move, or we'll work this out together when I get home." Lifting him from the dressing room table, and without thinking kissed his hard cheek.

"What are you doing?" Zakk stuttered.

"Oh, thought you might turn into a prince." She nervously giggled and stumbled out of the door.

"See you later, be careful," he yelled.

"Later," she called back, as her insides somersaulted in nervous excitement and cold dread.

Chapter Ten

"Break it up, girls." Mr. Thirtle held each girl at arm's length. Kiera threw random mime punches in the air, narrowly missing the weasly teacher's face.

"Chloe Wilson, Kiera Matthews, my office, *now*." Mrs. Jackson's voice boomed, like a foghorn.

"It's okay, Mrs. Jackson, I 'll deal with this," said Thirtle the ferret, in an enthused tone.

"Oh no, Mr. Thirtle, the pleasure will be all mine." leading the girls away, leaving Mr Thirtle looking on with envy. His nose twitched, and his beady eyes glared after them.

"So," continued the headmistress inside her office. "Who would like to go first?"

"Miss?" the girls chimed innocently.

"What in heaven's name is going on? Fancy picking a fight outside the staff room of all places." Mrs Jackson crossed her short arms, pushing her saggy chest up unnaturally high.

"She started it Miss," Chloe spat, shoving a finger within an inch of Kiera's face.

"You liar!" Kiera yelled.

Who would believe that this 'chalk and cheese' pair was once best friends? At nursery they'd share their sweets equally and held hands everywhere, even to the bathroom. Everything changed when at five-years-old the local newspaper, '*The Stanforth Scoop*', announced its search for a new carnival princess. Every mum, dad, and uncle entered their little darlings. When Kiera won it for a second year, Chloe stomped on Kiera's tiara; they never played together again. Kiera was beside herself, for the loss of her bosom buddy. She never cared about being carnival princess, and would've happily given the title to Chloe, if she'd asked for it. Now here they stood, like those two six-year-olds all those summers ago.

"She called me an orphan, and said I needed locking up!" Kiera crossed her arms tightly, to contain her anger.

"Now, Kiera, we'll have less of your outbursts thank you." Mrs Jackson uncrossed her arms, placing them on her hips. "In fact, you've not really been yourself all week. Is everything all right at home?"

"Yes, Miss, everything's fine," Kiera said, scowling at Chloe's smirking face.

"Well, I think you should both apologise and shake hands," cooed Mrs. Jackson. "Go on."

Chloe offered her hand out readily, sneering at Kiera.

"Kiera!" Mrs. Jackson ordered. Kiera begrudgingly shook the girl's hand.

"Sorry, Chloe," she mumbled.

"Me, too." Chloe smiled falsely, squeezing Kiera's fingers a little to hard.

"Thank you, Chloe, you may go."

As Chloe left the room, she mouthed the words, "you're dead," whilst the headmistress weebled back to her desk.

"I'm afraid, Kiera, that I am going to have to call your uncle," Mrs Jackson sighed.

"Please don't. I said I was sorry. I'll do better next time, promise." Not wanting Tom involved, she didn't want to disappoint him.

"This behaviour is getting worse, and you can offer no explanation. Disturbing classes, hiding in toilets, and now fighting. I wouldn't be doing my job if I just let it go. Your uncle can get to the bottom of it now." Mrs. Jackson's voice softened. "I'm worried about your studies. You'll ruin all your hard work if—" Stopping abruptly. "Kiera, will you stop humming when I'm talking to you. How very rude."

This time, Kiera caught herself doing it. It was like someone else making beautiful sounds. It made her feel warm and secure, like everything was going to be all right.

"That's it, young lady. I'm calling him right now. If I were you, I'd take a long hard look at yourself." She began to dial. "Oh hello, is that Mr. Matthews?"

* * * *

Maddy, Joe, and Daz sat in math class, bewildered, eagerly awaiting Kiera's return.

"Psst." Daz got Joe's attention and nodded toward the window. They watched Kiera herded to the car park by her uncle. He didn't look pleased.

"Uh-oh," sang Maddy.

"This doesn't look good," Joe stressed, as a note landed on his desk from Daz. It read, 'Kiera's after school? Find out what's going on. Yes? She shouldn't be alone. Something's definitely wrong.'

The three nodded in silent agreement, waiting for the bell to release them on their mission. What they didn't realise was that Kiera was far from alone. She had a whole other world watching out for her, in one way or another.

"You can go up if you like, but I doubt she'll want to see anyone," Tom said, letting the three confused faces pass him.

"Can you fill us in, Tom?" Joe asked.

"Afraid not kids, hoping you would tell me." Shaking his head, pushing his glasses up his nose. "Maybe you can get some sense out of her?"

They trundled up the stairs.

"Let me handle this," Maddy said in an authoritative tone. Stepping forward lightly tapping on the door. "Kiera sweetie, can we come in? We just wanna check you're all right."

* * * *

Kiera remained silent, sitting with her back propped against the door, tears welling.

"Why can't they just leave us alone," she whispered.

"Kiera," Joe intervened. "We're worried about you; will you let us in?"

"In more ways than one," Daz muttered. "Okay, I'll shut up."

"Put me in your bag, Kiera, I don't want them to see me. We can't trust anyone," Zakk instructed.

Kiera did so, wiped her eyes, and reached to unlock the door. Knowing her friends, they weren't about to give up easily.

"Right, that's it, I'm coming in," Daz shouted, barging through the door just as Kiera opened it. He landed on the bed, crashing into her fluffy pink pillows.

"Daz, you idiot," Maddy said, half laughing, half embarrassed.

"Get up, you dope."

"Guess you should all sit down," Kiera sighed. "He doesn't want me to say anything, but he doesn't know you like I do." They ran to take floor positions, like toddlers waiting for story time. Taking a deep breath, Kiera told them of the dreams, and how Zakk communicated through them. About him being a doll, and how she somehow was a special piece of the puzzle. The three were transfixed on the story, enthralled. When Kiera finished the tale, nobody spoke. Minutes passed while they stared everywhere but at each other.

Suddenly, thunderous laughter hammered through the silence. Daz rolled around in complete hysterics.

"Daz!" Maddy snapped in annoyance at her boyfriend's odd behaviour. "It's not funny. Pack it in."

Kiera's face burned an angry crimson. How could he react like this? She'd totally opened up, but now felt even more alone. Maybe Zakk was right. Maybe she could trust only him. Daz continued to behave like a tickled hyena.

"So, let's get this straight. You're telling us that you have a magic dolly...sorry, prince...from another world. Ha! Do you think we're stupid? Let's see it then!"

The floodgates had opened. Daz cried with nervous, uncontrollable laughter. Kiera marched across the room, nostrils flaring, and yanked the doll from her bag.

"There! You see!" Holding it up to each one in turn. Each looking at the doll skeptically. Even Joe looked unconvinced.

"Kiera, what are you doing?" Zakk asked.

"Proving that you're real. Speak, Zakk, tell them I'm not crazy." Silence. "For pity's sake, Zakk, tell them who you are!"

"It's no use, they cannot hear me. Only you can. For some reason

46

you are special, and you believe."

"What? You've got to be kidding me…" Mortified, she slumped onto the bed. The three friends looked on at this one-sided spectacle. Daz stared blankly for a while and then a smirk crossed his lips, followed by more mocking laughter.

"Sorry, sorry, but I can't, I can't breathe!" He rushed from the room, through the house into the garden below.

"I'm so sorry about that, Kiera, I really am," Maddy said, trying to console her friend and putting an arm around her. "I'm worried about you."

"Go after him, Madds." Kiera sighed.

"You sure?"

"I'll be fine, go."

"Okay, but I'll be right back." Maddy followed Daz out into the garden. Joe and Kiera stood frozen to the spot, staring at one another.

* * * *

"What was that?" the freckled red-head yelled at her soon to be 'ex-boyfriend.'

"Leave it," Daz yelled back. Terrence whimpered at Maddison's feet. "You need to calm down, you're scaring the mutt."

"And you need to stop acting like a total jerk," spat Maddy, her face becoming the same shade as her cherry Dr. Marten boots. "Your charming smile won't work this time. Do you realise you've made Kiera feel like complete poop! Our friend needs us, and you think it's okay to laugh at her?"

"Oh, come on, Madds, you don't actually believe all that tripe do ya? I mean, I know there's not much to do in this place except hang out.

But talking dolls…come on, what is she…five?" Daz softened his voice. "She just needs some time out from exams, and this talent comp means more to her than she's letting on. She'll be fine. Must be a girl thing…"

"You are sooo dumped, Daz Firth! Take your stupid sci-fi comics and your out of tune guitar and get lost!"

Daz didn't find this quite so funny now. "You want to split up? But I-I—"

"But you what? You're an un-feeling turd, and I can't forgive you." Tears leaking from her eyes, she turned away, swiftly walking inside.

Terrence barked Daz out of the gate.

"Yeah, thanks for the support, mate," he growled back at the little dog, slamming the gate behind him with warrior force.

* * * *

From the open window, Kiera had heard every word. She skirted past Joe, locking herself in the bathroom.

"Flipping great," Joe mumbled and followed. "Kiera, please come out. Let's talk about it. I want to believe you. I really do. But it's a big ask. Please, I'm serious, I want to believe."

"Me too," Maddy agreed, joining him outside the locked bathroom door.

"You do?" Kiera sprang to her feet. Opening the door, slowly peeping out.

"Aaahh, help! Kiera help me." Kiera's heart pounded as she ran to the bedroom.

"What is it?" Joe yelled, and the two followed behind.

"Zakk needs me. Oh. My. God!" Kiera gasped, open mouthed at

the scene unravelling before them. "Terrence! Get off at once!" Kiera ran toward the dog. Zakk was getting an all over tongue bath. If the little rescue dog had a full tail, he'd be wagging it with excitement.

"Get him off! It's disgusting! Dog meat breath, yuk!" Zakk squirmed.

The three friends broke into giggles. Joe bent to retrieve the doll from the dog's mouth.

"Thank you for your assistance," said Zakk, trying to shake off the slimy dog feeling.

"You're welcome," Joe replied. "Wait. What? No way!"

"You can hear me?" Zakk gasped.

"Yes, we can," Joe and Maddy duo-ed back.

"Oh- my- God." Maddy spoke slowly, turning a little pale.

"Perhaps you both opened up to the possibility, because of your love for Kiera." Zakk suggested.

"Then you really do believe? And I'm not crazy!" cried Kiera; hugging her shocked, speechless friends tightly, feeling not quite as alone.

"Zakk!" yelled Kiera, jumping over the bed and almost flying across the room. "Please wake up, don't be gone!" Shaking the doll vigorously.

"Please stop it! I may lose a few brain cells." Zakk rubbed his shiny head.

"Thank God, I thought you'd turned fully plastic."

"Of course not," Zakk said, "But, thanks for the massive headache."

"But it's Friday, your birthday! We fell asleep and never came up with a plan to stop the Witch Queen."

"Err, slow down. Breathe. It's Thursday. I won't turn into a doll fully until seven o'clock tomorrow night, the exact time I was born. Until now I've been biding time, but time seems unwilling to wait for me. I keep trying to come up with a plan but being trapped like this and without my men behind me...I'm still clueless," he sighed. "I'm sorry that you have been dragged into this mess. If you can just assist me to the vortex, I will do the rest..."

"What? I don't think so! *We* will both go after school," Kiera said, in her most assertive voice. "We'll fight the witch together and get your world and body back." Zakk looked impressed for a second. "Just wondering, how do we get to your world exactly?" Kiera asked. "And what's a vortex?"

"There is a gateway, a vortex to my dimension, hidden in your school car park." Zakk paused. "The thing is, Kiera, whatever happens whilst you're passing through it, don't panic. Stay calm, don't lose your head. I mean that literally. It's been known that you can go in one way and come out completely different."

"Huh?" Kiera scratched her head. "The more I hear, the more confusing it all seems."

"Apparently," Zakk continued, "old tales tell of a pixie and a Grenadine beast going into the vortex together and exiting as one big beastie mess."

"Yeah right, I'm not as stupid as you look you know!" Half laughing. "Whatever, I'm not scared," she said, unable to make eye-contact, keeping her true feelings hidden. "Looks like we're going after school then. Maybe take the other ring while the witch sleeps or something, and before you know it, you're a prince again."

"If only it were that simple." He sighed.

* * * *

"Are you sure you'll be okay in there?" Kiera whispered, trying to avoid the hives of kids flooding their way.

"Positive, you've made it very cozy, thanks." Zakk sat back, resting on Kiera's gloves.

"Okay. I'll lock you in; I'll be back to check on you at break time." She hovered.

"Will you just go? You're making me nervous." Zakk said.

Kiera closed the locker door.

Now left in the darkness with just his thoughts, he had to come up with a plan before tonight.

* * * *

"Hello, can I help you?" Tom got up from behind the counter where he'd been sipping tea and reading the local paper. The customer didn't acknowledge him and carried on gliding around the store.

"No no," she muttered to herself. "This won't do!"

"Are you looking for something special?" Tom raised his voice, stepping forward.

"Yes, I am actually." She turned to stare at him, almost as if he was being nosey. "I'm looking for a present for…for my niece."

"Well, let's see," Tom said. "We have some lovely books and—"

"No no," the woman said, rudely cutting in. "I'm thinking more of a doll."

He'd never seen anyone like her. Tall and wiry; with black, slick hair and the emptiest eyes he'd ever had the misfortune to look upon. For a moment, feeling pity for her. She rifled through the small selection of dolls, tossing them quickly to the side.

"Uh-huh," Tom cleared his throat. "Perhaps if I knew your niece's age?"

"I want a boy doll," she demanded.

"Now it just so happens, I have one left in the back." He left for a few seconds and returned with the doll. "This is it." Presenting an Action Man. "It's on sale. Only four pounds, ninety-nine," hoping the she'd take it and leave. The waspish woman snatched it from him, staring at it intently.

"No! That's not it," she yelped, throwing it onto the counter.

Tom became agitated. The 'customer's always right' scenario seemed to vacate his head.

"Are you the only person who works here?" the rude woman asked.

"My niece does occasionally. Why?"

"No reason. Is she in today?"

"No." Tom kept it short and to the point, where Kiera was concerned, she was his business only.

"Are there any other toy shops in the area?"

"No, there's one a few miles up the coast," he said, without saying which direction she should take.

"Well, I may be back." Her response sounded more like a threat.

Tom opened the door, and she glided through. He slammed it behind her. *We may be closed*, he smiled to himself.

"So, what you gonna do? I mean, it's like world-changing stuff. Pretty major if you ask me," Maddy probed. "You want me to come with you? I mean, have you even got a plan?"

"No, I'm feeling pretty useless…I mean, what can I possibly do to help? I'm just old enough to get a paper round, how the heck am I supposed to fight an evil witch? And thanks for the offer, but Zakk doesn't even want me helping. Let's just change the subject," Kiera said. The two girls headed toward the school canteen. "So, how's life without Daz? Has he called or texted you?"

"No, nothing," Maddy replied, with a heavy frown.

"It's all my fault isn't it?"

"Don't be stupid! It's his fault for being such an utter plonker," Maddy replied, rolling her eyes.

"Wait." Kiera stopped, grabbing Maddy's bag, nearly ripping her arm out of its socket. "I nearly forgot, I said I'd check on Zakk. All this boy talk, and I forgot the most important one!"

"Joe?" suggested Maddy, one brow raised.

"No, you great plum." Although thinking about it, she hadn't seen Joe all day. They usually walked to school together, but today he didn't come around. She figured he had a sports thing, or something. She would call him after school, if he didn't appear within the next few hours.

"Can we grab lunch first? I can almost taste the food from here. Please, can't think on an empty stomach. I'm so hungry I could eat my own feet."

"Oh, go on then, but ten minutes tops." Kiera shook her head and Maddison steered her toward the canteen line, after which they ate in silence for a while.

"You're into this Zakk, aren't you?"

"No!" Kiera laughed, nearly spitting out a chip.

"So, why you blushing like you've been caught naked in the school pool?"

"I'm not," Kiera snapped. "A chip went down the wrong hole, that's all."

"Whatever you say mate, whatever you say." Maddy laughed. "Can we slow down? I'm getting indigestion. It's not as if Zakk can open the locker and jump out."

"Two minutes, then I'm gone." Kiera loved her friend dearly, but speed was not in her vocabulary.

"Talking of boys," Maddy gobbled a burger, "we seem to be missing a 'Daz' today, too." Scanning the canteen to see if the gothic, broody guy would cross their radar.

"Yep," Kiera agreed. "We are lacking in the Daz department, not that you're bothered, right?" Maddy looked away. "Maybe he's really upset about you dumping him. He does really care about you, you know. So, we are a Daz down, and the lovely Joe is nowhere to be seen. Hmm, the plot thickens. So, can we check Zakk now please?"

"I'm waiting for you, slow coach," Maddy teased, finishing her milkshake and collecting her stuff. "I will take him back, once he's begged a lot. Guess I miss him a bit." Maddy shrugged.

"Do you think they're together, the boys I mean?"

"Why, you jealous, Matthews?" Maddy laughed. "Come on, you're in a hurry, aren't you? Let's go find your prince." The girls linked arms and marched down the corridor.

* * * *

"Ssooo, you ssay you have ssomething that Her Highnesss isss ssearching for?" Googe slimed closer. "Give it to me; I'll make ssure sshe getsss it."

"No thanks. For some reason, I don't trust you. I'll give it to her myself," answered the defiant informer.

"Oh, but I inssissst." Googe held out his stubby, green hand.

"Sssoo do I," mimicked the informer. "Are you trying to be comical all the way down there? I could pull you apart like the worm you are and feed you to the crows."

"I could end you right now." Googe grabbed the tormentor. "But My Queen would be mossst disspleasssed."

The informer laughed mockingly. "You mean, you're not allowed to make any decisions."

"Well now," replied a crumpled Googe. "Which isss it to be, the prince, the ring or the girl? One and you've ssaved yoursssself from certain death, two and you may even get your freedom back, and a hat trick might just ssave the one you love." Googe smiled, knowing he'd hit a nerve.

"How dare you talk about my life, you too, are a slave, or did you forget?" The informer pushed Googe to the ground, wanting to finish him off right there.

"No." Googe quickly jumped up. "But I enjoy my work. I get to deal with gutter life like yoursssself."

"I will no longer deal with the puppet, only the master."

"We sshall ssee about that." Googe smirked. A sonic boom broke the skies. The informer's bones rattled; their muscles tensed. This sound had been heard once before, as a child on that horrible day, when their world changed forever. At a very young age they had witnessed this same looming shadow in the sky, after which the explosions came. A demonic shrieking and fire everywhere. The informer never knew which took their parents, the beast or the flames. They just knew that day; nothing would ever be the same again.

"You remember your old friend, Albatron?" Googe chortled.

The informer's silhouette shook, as the vast darkness of the almighty beast overhead, eclipsed them.

* * * *

"Where is he? Where is he?" Kiera squealed like a pig with burnt trotters. Kids and teachers came to a stand still around her. She rummaged through the locker. Books, pencils, and gum flew past Maddy's head.

"Okay, mate," Maddy said, glancing around at the unwanted attention. "Be cool, keep calm."

"He's not here," Kiera said, grabbing Maddy's shoulders before turning back to the empty locker.

"Are you sure he was? You've been under a lot of pressure lately," Maddy said, rubbing her friend's arm. "Maybe you left him at home?" Kiera spun and stared at her best friend.

"You." Kiera mouthed. "You already knew Zakk wouldn't be here, didn't you? Did you take him? He warned me not to trust anyone."

"What? No, you've got it wrong! I just want to help you," Maddy whimpered.

"That day we met—it was no accident was it? She sent you to watch me."

"No, Kiera, calm down. Think about what you're saying," Maddy begged, tears ready to burst from her eyes.

Kiera cringed at the hurt expression on Maddy's face. *What the hell am I saying? Maybe I am losing the plot! I can't be sure...can't be sure...has Zakk gone without me? Thinking it's for my own good? How did he break out of the locker?*

"God, Maddison, I'm so sorry, I can't think straight …I—I just need to be alone for a while…" Kiera swiftly turned and scurried away—away from the spies, the liars, and the prying eyes.

Chapter Fourteen

Kiera sat in the office once again. Staring blankly at numerous certificates hanging on the walls, hiding the torment inside. How could she save Zakk now? She couldn't even keep him safe. Who was *for* her and who was against? She couldn't enter the talent contest if Zakk were to die, and then Uncle Tom would have questions why she didn't sing, and the unbelievable truth would come out. If Zakk were to die…the word 'die' repeated on her like a bad curry. A sudden rush of warmth glowed within. An inner peace calmed her. Unable to explain it, she knew Zakk wasn't dead, that somehow, they were connected. She could still feel his presence, like an old coat wrapped around her. Why her though? Why not Lyra Chidwick, or Karen Dillon, or one of the other girls at school?

"Why me?" Kiera said out loud.

"Kiera, what do you mean by that?" asked the weebly headteacher, Mrs. Jackson. Kiera snapped back to reality.

"Err, what?"

"Do you want some time alone with your uncle?" Mrs. Jackson enquired.

Kiera shrugged.

"Well, I would like some time with you, young lady." Uncle Tom appeared in the doorway. *Busted*, Kiera thought, as his nostrils flared in a quiet rage. Mrs. Jackson left the room.

"I'm sorry." Kiera jumped up before he could speak.

"I'm sorry too, Kiera, that your behaviour is out of order and frankly, quite bizarre. It has to stop; do you understand?" Tom's tone softened. "Why won't you let me help you? You know you can tell me anything."

Kiera studied him. *Did he know? Was he in on it too?* Shaking her head, disbelieving the paranoid voices trying to take over her sanity. Tom looked broken.

"Is it Joe?" he asked. "Have you two squabbled? Is that what all the nonsense was about at home the other day?"

She couldn't believe how far off the mark he was. Uncle Tom could normally read her like a book, but this time her pages remained tightly shut. *It's for his own good,* she told herself. After losing just about everybody else; she couldn't lose Tom too. Maddy could be a double agent, but now that idea just sounded stupid. Daz thought she was a crazy loon, and Joe, her oldest and dearest friend, was missing. Who knows what could have happened? Tom was the only root left, keeping her earthbound and levelheaded. She couldn't lose that, not now.

After the drive home in total silence, they got out of Tom's green Beetle, slamming the doors in unison.

"We need a chat." Tom nodded toward the kitchen. She followed him through the house, head down, like a puppy that had been caught chewing its master's slipper. "Take a seat." Tom folded his arms. Kiera sat down at the table, idly playing with the salt pot. She would listen to whatever he had to say and agree to do better next time. Then make her excuses, ring Joe, and find Zakk. The thought of facing the vortex alone left her reeling inside. Wanting so much to ask Tom to help, but sadly that wasn't an option. She hadn't even thought of facing the Witch Queen, or if it were possible to even return home again. Zakk was all that mattered right now. She could sense the connection to him calling out to her. *But why me?*

"I'm sending you to your Granny Bertine's," Tom sighed.

"What!" Kiera leapt from the table knocking over the salt pot. "Great, more bad luck, that's all I need."

"Just for the summer holidays, just for a change of scenery. It'll do you the world of good," he said, in a very matter of fact way. "You're not going to get your own way this time. I've been far too soft on you in the past. I just want the old Kiera back."

"Okay," she nodded. "I will go at the weekend, after school's finished." This way, she would know Zakk's fate, good or bad, it would all be over. After all, she may not even survive to see Saturday. Her whole body tensed at the thought.

"No, young lady, you will go today. There's a three-fifty train, and I want you on it."

"I can't, I can't!" Panic boiled upward from her toes, erupting in her head.

"Why?" Tom snapped. "What's so important that you wouldn't want to see your gran? All your tests are finished for the year; there's no valid reason."

"Well," Kiera stammered. "Joe, he may be sick. I need to be here for him, and there's the talent competition. I couldn't let Madam Swift down."

"But you can let me down?" Tom said, a frown line appearing down the centre of his forehead. "Your bag is packed, get your coat, we're leaving in two minutes."

Kiera's eyes strained to fight the hot tears caressing her cheeks. Catching the sadness on her uncle's face before he turned and walked away.

Upstairs, she called Joe to ask for help. Whilst tapping his home number, a numb sensation fell upon her.

"Is Joe there, Mrs. Crosby? …You haven't heard from him since this morning? No, he hasn't been with me. I'm sure he'll turn up; he's probably gone to the gym or something. I guess we've just been missing each other all day. Yes, I'll tell him to call you if he comes here. Okay, bye." Putting the phone down, Kiera paused. Her brain switched off for a few moments. Unable to take in all that was happening. *Where's Joe?* Instinct told her he was in trouble, and that she was somehow to blame.

* * * *

"Well what happened to you?" the Witch Queen huffed, looking at Googe's bloodstained face.

"It wasss the informant, My Queen, but believe me, they came off far worssse."

"Oh yes?" she smiled, unconvinced.

"Yesss, My Queen. I had to re-introduce them to your pet, they ssoon backed down."

"Good, Googey, good. Now, do you have a little present for me? Something to decorate my beautiful finger perhaps?" Cocking her head to the side in a child-like manner.

"No, My Queen. They wanted to give you their findingsss in persssson." Googe lowered his slanted eyes.

"Well, they better bring it soon. The clock is tick-tocking, tick-tocking." Turning, swishing her cloak, dramatically. "I'm off back to the sea-side." She hollered. "I have some shopping to do." With that, she left in a white blaze of light, highlighting a pile of discarded hollow dolls.

Chapter Fifteen

"Just go." Kiera anxiously drummed her fingers on the glass as her uncle paced the platform. "Just go!" she roared, to the astonishment of the other passengers in the carriage. A businessman shuffled his over-large newspaper in annoyance, whilst a mother shushed a young boy who sniggered and pointed. Quite oblivious to it all, Kiera just wanted her stubborn uncle to leave. She was doing as she was told, what more did he want?

The train started chugging, and the guard yelled something incomprehensible. What now? Kiera panicked as her uncle waved solemnly. For a second, Kiera felt she'd failed him. He walked away toward the exit of the station. His head low, shoulders drooped.

The train gently rocked along its tracks. Without a second thought, Kiera sprang to her feet, sprinted down the carriage, hitting the emergency stop button. Zakk's life was at stake, maybe even Joe's. This was much more important than the bewildered passengers and angry ranting of the conductor, who was quickly descending upon her. She swung the door open and made a gigantic leap to catch the very edge of the platform. Panic pin-balled up her spine, but she hung on, legs clanging together like wind chimes.

"Owww," she cried out. Face hitting the concrete edge and scraping both elbows. Wishing she'd thought this through, gripping hard onto the side of the platform, overlooking the dark, hard, pit of the tracks. Gasps of horror floated out from inside the train.

"Hang on there, Miss," shouted a roly-poly guard who was huffing and puffing his way over the bridge above.

"Don't move, Miss!" shouted a second guard.

"Matthews, what the heck are you doing?" A pair of familiar green eyes bored down upon her, followed by a manic grin.

"Oh God, not now." Kiera grimaced. *Ben Wilson of all people!* "Well help me up then. I can't hold on much longer."

"Please?" Ben jeered.

"Please. Please!" she pleaded. Ben put out his hand. Kiera attempted to grab it. He withdrew it.

"Ben!"

"I'll pull you up, if you let my sister win the talent competition." Ben shook his head at her predicament. "If only I had a camera."

"Whatever. Just get me up!" Just then, the guards appeared.

"Move, kid, don't just stand there." The larger man pushed him to the side. After watching the two men winch her up, Ben ran from the station laughing. She knew news of this unfortunate incident would hit school-wide before long. Kiera got to her feet and dusted herself down.

"Let's get you inside," puffed the fat, red-faced man.

"No, I've got to go. Thanks anyway." Kiera hobbled from the station toward the taxi rank. She had to get back to the house and find the ring—the only thing left to barter with.

"Fourteen Pearce Drive, please." The taxi drove past Tom's shop. She was astonished to see a sign in the window, which read, 'Closed until further notice.'

What was going on? He never mentioned closing, especially not this close to tourist season. Kiera's mouth was as dry as Terrence's bone, both palms itched in anticipation.

"Can you drop me off a block before please?" The driver nodded. The cab came to a halt, and they sat in silence. Should she go in and face up to Uncle Tom, or sneak in the house without detection? *Maybe if I live through this, I'll explain it all then.*

"That'll be two-ninety then." The driver's bloodshot eyes gazed from his mirror to look at her. Throwing a five-pound note at him, she exited the cab.

"Keep the change."

"Thanksss, Misss," hissed the driver. She couldn't quite see his eyes under his cap. A cold sensation snaked her spine. The taxi drove away. Kiera tried to stay calm and focus. Darting in and out of hedges, like a hunted deer, until arriving at her destination.

Terrence yelped when she stuck her head through the dog flap, sizing up if she could perhaps slither through. Staying low, she could avoid confrontation.

"Shhh, daft dog, shhh!" Terrence bounded forward giving her a swift lashing of wet tongue. "Eeeww!" squealed Kiera, automatically forcing her head out of the tiny door. "Gross! Busted by a dog." She leaned against the back door, wondering what to do next. The door swung open, causing her to stumble backward. *How odd.* Uncle Tom was always so tight about security.

"Err, hello," Kiera called out. "Uncle Tom?" Walking cautiously from room to room, wary of what she might find. At best, Tom would be there to read the riot act. At worst, she shuddered not wanting to think of what could've happened to him. Tentatively pushing the last door open, her bedroom. *Something's very wrong.*

"Err, hello?" No one was there but Terrence, who shadowed her obediently. All was pristine just as she'd left it. Kiera frantically emptied cupboards and drawers, until her whole room looked like a crime scene. "Where did I put it? Where did I put the stupid thing?" Terrence growled as items whizzed by him. "Shush, Terrence, I need to think." Collapsing onto the bed, hands behind her head, trying to think back to the night this mess started. "My jeans pocket!" she yelped, blazing across the landing to the bathroom laundry basket. Rummaging to the bottom as Terrence played dodge ball with various socks and briefs. "Phew." Pulling the jeans out, sliding a hand into the pocket.

The warmth of the ring touched her fingertips, and she clenched it tightly. "At last, some luck for our team." She smiled. Shoving the ring onto her finger, turning to leave. A dark figure eclipsed the doorway. Kiera screamed and jumped back. A strange being, a little shorter than she, blocked her passage like a goalkeeper. She touched the ring nervously. An overwhelming feeling of strength came over her. *I can take him in a fight.*

The creature stepped into the light, which did him no favours. His slanted eyes darted from her face, to the ring, and back again. Like the duels she'd seen in old black and white movies, she knew someone had to draw first.

"Going ssomewhere?" he asked, charging, knocking her backward into the toilet.

"Who are you?" Kiera spat. Placing both hands down on the toilet seat, pushing herself up.

"I am the great Googe. And you, Princesss, have ssomething I want." He grabbed for the ring as Kiera stepped back. "I knew it wasss you. Who needsss sspiesss, when you can do the job yourssself? I'm sso clever. It took many yearsss, of courssse, but I made it my misssion. Sso you're her? The famousss chossen one…I wasss expecting ssomeone a little sstronger, ssomeone sspecial…"

"What? What are you talking about? Chosen one? It's not me!" Kiera tried to make a break for it.

"I don't think sso, Misssy." He twisted her arm around her back, trying to snatch the ring. They struggled. "It'sss you, you'll figure it out or maybe you wont. Maybe you're a bit sstupid…the prophecy didn't cover that part…"

"What prophecy? You're crazy. Why are you doing this?" she pleaded, arm twisted in pain.

"I will do anything to be My Queen'sss number one. I will be by her sside through her reign, until time runsss out. I will be in hisstory booksss, while you will just be hisstory!"

Her opponent was a lot stronger than she gave him credit for. Any moment the ring would be his.

"Oh, Zakk," she cried. "I'm so sorry."

A faint humming eclipsed the room. Kiera recognised the tune. The ring shot a beam of multicoloured light into Googe's eyes, temporarily blinding the creature.

"What did you do to me? What magic iss thisss!" The Lizard-like foe screamed out, shielding his eyes.

Terrence bounded in, knocking the intruder off his huge feet. Like a lion with raw flesh, the dog was not letting go. Googe hissed, writhing in pain. Kiera gave the little terrier a thankful head rub.

"I guess you'll always be just a number two," she said, stepping over the intruder. With that, she grabbed her blades and fled.

"She's here, you'd better come quickly." The school counsellor panicked, listening for a response. "No, I don't know. Well, she's just standing in the car park, frozen to the spot. The poor thing looks completely lost." She waited for directions. "I will, yes of course I'll watch her. Do you think...?" Ms. Watson's voice trailed off, as she didn't really need an answer.

"Yes," replied the voice at the end of line. "It's happening; Kiera's going in. *"*

* * * *

Kiera's mind now rejected all knowledge or reason. Staring at Joe's bike, crumpled on the ground. Now fearing something terrible had happened to him. Every time she tried to urge herself on, her feet held fast to the spot. Kiera's hand sprang involuntarily forward, the ring on her finger pulsated. Like a magnet, it drew out a whirl of grey mass, which swam and flickered into a roaring fog. The ring was a key as well as a bargaining tool, to get Zakk's freedom back.

"So, you must be the mighty vortex. You're not so scary." Shivering, remembering Zakk's tales of weird mutations. "Well I guess I'm already a freak, so you can't change me much," Kiera muttered, slugging toward the fierce gateway. The closer she came, the more her body temperature dropped—her toes and fingers tingled with numbness, her lips stiffened. Her eyes felt sore at the harsh, bitter cold. Unable to catch a breath, she panicked. Mind racing, like she was falling through space and time. Brown hair whipped around her face; the chill of the air lashed at all senses. Now face-to-face with it, she felt faint and fell to the ground. Pulling herself along on her hands and knees, until she was a safe distance away.

"Kiera? Are you okay?" A voice behind startled her. It was Ms. Watson. She bent down, putting her hand out to pull Kiera up. "If you take a run at it, you'll hardly notice you're in it." Ms. Watson smiled.

"Huh?" Kiera replied. "You can see it? You can see the vortex?" Ms. Watson nodded, chewing her bottom lip. "Who are you?" Kiera fumed. "You're one of them!"

"Yes, I am, but I'm on your side, I promise." Ms. Watson placed a hand on Kiera's shoulder. Kiera saw truth in her eyes.

"You could've helped before now, instead of watching me fail. I needed help…"

"We weren't sure if it was happening at first, we prayed it wasn't. I couldn't help you. I promised I'd leave it to—" She stopped abruptly.

"You promised who? Who did you promise, Ms. Watson? Tell me."

"Kiera." The woman grabbed her tightly. "We haven't time for whys and wherefores. Zantar's future is in your hands. You need to get your skates on."

"My skates!" Kiera untied the blades hanging from her shoulders like a scarf. "I'll skate through it!" She fumbled with the laces. "That way, I'll gain enough speed to break through the pain. Come with me?"

"Sadly, I cannot. My post is here, and this journey is yours." Ms. Watson stepped back. "You can do this, Kiera."

Kiera got to her feet. *I can do it. Zakk, Joe, I'm coming for you.* She skated to the far end of the car park to gain speed. One foot started to rev, like a motorbike, standing opposite the mysterious, swirling gateway, willing herself to go on.

"Go, Kiera!" Ms. Watson shouted. Kiera pushed off hard.

Accelerating, flying past Ms. Watson like a winged whippet. No time to stop or think, she held her breath and closed her eyes. Ms. Watson's cries stopped. Nothingness consumed her. Electricity crackled through her body, she contorted three hundred and sixty degrees into the air, plummeting toward the ground. Smacking down hard. Sprawled out like a broken puppet, laying motionless for a few seconds.

Gasping hard, her eyes opened wide. It hurt to lift her head up. Giving herself a quick once over. She was still in one piece, dazed, bloody and aching from the wrath of the vortex. Kiera slowly sat up and scanned the surroundings. Yes, she'd made it but made it where? This surely couldn't be the blissful Zantar that Zakk adored so much. The place of wonderment and great light that appeared in her dreams, was really this soul-destroying, black world, cold, hard and barren. Sparse of any life it seemed. Everything lost, dying, bereft of beauty. Trees from her dreams that once shimmered drops of silver and lilac, now drooped like a frown. The pastel painted skies were now a charcoaled smudge. Zantar's heart had been ripped away.

Kiera scrambled to stand, but her blades collided with the rocks, she fell, cutting both knees upon landing. Her blood amplified its brightness, against the grey, dying backdrop. Even the weather seemed to have abandoned this place. Nothing was welcome here.

Wiping her leg, trying to be strong and go on. Off came the blades, Kiera started out barefoot across the rocky unknown.

"Ow, ow!" she cried in painful frustration as the rocks bit at her heels. "Zakk, you'd better be here; this is all for you." Tears ran down her cheeks. A quiet, unknown force, however, drove her onward. Kiera was the key, she couldn't understand it, but believed enough to risk her life. The dreams, the strange connection with Zakk. The feeling that she'd been here before. "There must be a reason." She forced back the building tears. The rocks seem to have no end. Each becoming sharper and angrier as she clumsily jumped from one to another. Her throat was dry, her limbs sore, and every bone ached. Crying out when a rock edge sliced her skin.

A tiny bark pierced the air. Kiera jumped. There, a few rocks behind, stood Terrence. Somehow, the little dog had followed her through the vortex and was pawing his way through the uneven ground, running to catch up. Kiera scooped him up in her arms, burying her face in his matted fur.

"I am so glad to see you, little one. Don't know how you got here, but I'm sure glad of the company."

Chapter Seventeen

"So, you're saying you had the girl and the ring in your grasp, and you let them get away!" The Witch Queen's rage boomed over the palace, shaking fear into all who were left alive.

"Sso, sso, ssorry, Your Majesssty," Googe whimpered, as he 'hedge-hogged' into a ball at her feet.

"I should throw you to the D'rogs and let them teach you some obedience. You let a girl, a little girl, beat you?"

"Your Highnesss, pleassse, sshe had a mighty pet, a huge creature!" Googe lied. "They cornered me, believe me, Oh Great One."

"Hmmm, so she has a beast, does she?" The Witch Queen flustered for a second. "No matter, I will crush her and her ill-advised pet. Get up you fool. Get Albatron ready. I sense our informant is on their way, and I feel there may be a little gift for me. Send Alby to bring them here a little faster; time is not waiting for us."

"Yesss, Your Royalnesss, thank you." Googe bowed repeatedly.

"And, Googe, put extra security on all the exits. Once I have my prince, this time I'm keeping him."

* * * *

Kiera halted. "My God," she sighed. "How are we supposed to get across that?" Looking across at the next, even bigger canyon of razor-like rocks. It was deep and vast. She could barely see beyond it. Terrence barked at her heels, urging her onward. "Come on then, boy, if you think we can." Feeling exhausted, picking up the little no-tailed terrier. For a rescue dog that she'd only known a few weeks, his commitment was astounding. Making their way down into the canyon, each rock felt trickier than the next. Kiera hopped from one to the other, slipping occasionally. Her feet were cut to ribbons, her lips begged for water. Eventually reaching the other side but encountered a daunting climb out that seemed almost vertical.

"Come on, boy, we can do this."

Terrence cocked his head, as if to ask 'why?' She focused all thoughts on Zakk, and grabbed at the gravelled, muddy rock-face. Each time taking one step upward and sliding two steps down. The air grew cooler as evening chased behind. Terrence managed to scramble to the top, after many attempts, yapping with encouragement.

All energy drained. Kiera only had a little way to go. "I can't do it! I can't do it, Terrence," she sobbed, clinging onto the rock-face. "You win, you win!" Her body now covered in mud and blood. Exhausted, sinking her head into her arms, hanging on for dear life.

"That's not the girl I know. She's no quitter!" A familiar voice called from the wilderness above.

"Joe?" Kiera's head shot up. He was kneeling next to Terrence on the cliff edge, smiling down. Unlike Kiera though, he looked pretty clean. "What are you—? How did you—?"

"Let's get you up here first." She'd never been so happy to see him. She should have known Joe would never desert her. Stretching as tall as her tiny frame would allow. He finally managed to grab her hands, pulling her up. Safely by his side, Kiera clung to him for as long as possible, taking comfort in his arms.

"Steady now, you'll get people talking," Joe grinned.

"Oh, Joe, how the heck did you get here? Why did you come? Why?"

"Isn't it obvious?" Joe replied, blushing. "But let's focus on the job at hand."

"How did you make it through the vortex?"

"I followed *it*. I just did what *it* did."

"It? What, Joe? What did you follow? A person? Someone we know?" A feeling of dread washed over Kiera.

"It was. It was—" Joe stammered, further alarming her.

Please not Maddy…Please not her. Kiera prayed.

"It's Ben Wilson, isn't it?" Kiera interjected. "He's the spy; him and that Chloe have always hated me."

"No, Kiera," said a soft voice behind. "It's me."

Chapter Eighteen

"You!" Kiera's head buzzed with confusion.

"Don't do it, man! Put the doll down," Joe said calmly, edging forward.

Kiera's heart raced upon watching her 'friend' flick on a lighter and hold it up toward Zakk. The amber flecks in Daz's topaz eyes danced angrily.

"Please," Kiera pleaded. "Whatever's going on, we can sort it out."

"Kiera, help me." Zakk's voice was faint. She could feel him slipping away. "The heat...I can't take it."

"Daz, you're hurting him. He'll melt. Stop it!" Kiera yelled.

"Damn doll won't shut up. Jabbered on... the whole journey. Full of pleading and false promises. Good riddance I say." Daz moved the flame closer to Zakk.

"Goodbye Kiera," Zakk whispered, giving in to the oncoming furnace. Kiera sobbed.

"Right, that's it, Firth. You're going down!" Joe took a run at his rival. Flying through the night like a comet, hitting his target with an almighty crash. Zakk was catapulted a few metres away in the scuffle. The boys fought and rolled, like wild tigers. Kiera scooped Zakk up, holding on so tightly.

"Zakk, are you all right?"

Zakk said nothing. The doll was cold. Was she too late?

Daz punched Joe in the face. He got to his feet to dust himself down as Joe swept both legs from under him. The two boys lay panting, like dehydrated dogs. Kiera's tears fell on the plastic prince she cradled. Taking some comfort that she could still sense Zakk's presence, even if their connection was weakened. The three sat in silence. Terrence barked wildly at Daz.

"That dog never liked me," Daz scowled.

"You of all people! We trusted you." Joe got up, making his way over to Kiera.

"Why, Daz?" Kiera choked on the tears. "Why you doing this?" Her gaze fell on his torn clothing and the bloody claw mark on his arm. "What's happened to you?"

"Why are you bothered with him? He's not one of us. You're not even human, are you?" Joe spat, putting his arm around Kiera for protection.

"I'm just...I'm just..." Daz whispered. A single tear pinched its way free, sitting defiantly on his cheek.

"You're just what? An evil traitor!" Joe spat. His usual 'happy-go-lucky' manner had disappeared; his brows knitting an angry frown across his forehead.

"No, I'm just a slave." Daz sighed. "The Witch Queen commands me. She has my—" Daz stopped abruptly.

"She has your what?" Kiera urged. She needed more than he was giving, none of this made any sense. This was Daz, part of the gang, part of her family.

"She has my sister. If I don't deliver the prince, she'll kill her." Daz shuddered.

"Daz," Kiera spoke softly, holding onto Zakk for dear life; nothing would separate them again. If necessary, she'd take Daz on herself. But she knew him. This was Daz who carried her to the nurse's office when she twisted an ankle in gym class. Daz who wrote daft songs for Maddy and sang like a cat caught in a bath.

"I know you, you're a really good person. But you must see that if the Witch Queen gets Zakk, she will rule this world and not just your sister will suffer."

"But she promised. She said she'd let us both go if I just did this one thing...God I'm such an idiot." Daz sighed. "I always thought it was you, Kiera, from the moment we met I knew you were special. But I grew to like you so damn much. Why'd you have to be so great? I couldn't give you up, but I cannot stall her any longer. Take the prince. I won't try to stop you." Daz stepped back to give them a clear pathway.

"Thank you, I know how hard this must be, but we must..." Kiera was silenced by the deafening shrieking overhead. They looked up in horror at the winged metal beast nose-diving toward them.

"Go!" Daz ordered. "Run, you idiots! Save yourselves! Save us all!"

Joe grabbed Kiera's elbow. "Come on, you heard him."

"No, Daz, come with us." Kiera clutched Zakk to her heart, grabbing for Daz with her free hand.

"Go! Go now! The beast has come for me, go while you still can." Daz pushed her away. "Promise you'll help my sister?"

Kiera nodded, unable to form words. Joe ripped her away from the shadow of the mighty Albatron.

Daz turned slowly to face his fate.

"Don't look back," Joe ordered as the metal bird flew overhead. In its iron talons, Daz's limp body dangled. Kiera stopped running, gasping for breath.

"Do you think he's—?"

"No." Joe huffed. "I don't think anything. I need to focus on keeping us alive. You're all that matters, okay?" Kiera felt surprised, a little impressed at this strong, authoritative side of Joe. Relief swept through her; at last she was no longer alone.

He scanned the area. "Look over there, through that pathway of trees. There's some sort of palace. Do you think it's hers?"
Kiera squinted, there in the distance stood a tall black spindly palace. Its sharp turrets seemed to stretch and disappear into the colourless skies above. An eerie mist shrouded the structure. The night sky around it seemed denser somehow, like a warning to all, not to approach.

"I know it is," Kiera shuddered, knowing she had to go on. Fate gave her no choice.

* * * *

"We have the traitor, Your Majesssty," Googe smiled in triumph.

"And do we have the prince?" The witch's cold, dead eyes burnt in anticipation.

"Alasss no, Your Greatnesss. The boy gave it to her."

"What!" The queen roared, and the whole of Zantar shook.

* * * *

Kiera and Joe were thrown to the ground.

"What was that?" Kiera gasped.

"Dunno." Joe pulled Kiera to her feet. "Some sort of quake? Are you okay?"

"Yes, I'm fine. I'm tougher than I look you know." Kiera smiled.

"Come on then, 'Supergirl,' let's do this." Joe placed his hand in hers and they faced the ghostly path of trees, cautiously walking between them.

"They're so ugly now. More like skeletons of themselves. Such a shame." Kiera mused.

"How do you know? Been here on vacation?" Joe joked, keeping his focus on the unknown pathway stretching before them.

"Maybe," Kiera shrugged. "Or, maybe I've dreamt all this."

"No time for exploring that..." Joe's grasp tightened as the trees were starting to look less like trees and more like bony, skeletal hands. Sounds of twigs crunching and bark breaking became clearer. The trees along the pathway, morphed clumsily into menacing weapons.

"Do you see that? Or is my mind playing tricks on me?" Kiera whispered. The two froze in horror as the giant hands formed fists and swung their way.

"Run, Kiera!"

Their feet pounded hard on the ground and the mighty fists swung forward, like demolition balls. Joe pulled Kiera onward, weaving them both in and out through the oncoming threat.

"Nearly there," Joe called over his shoulder. Kiera stumbled on a rock, dropping Zakk in the process. "Come on!" Joe pulled her arm as she swooped, picking up the silent prince. "Go!" Joe pushed her forward as a wooden hand lunged for him, thumping hard into his chest. Kiera looked on in horror. His eyes fixed helplessly on hers, before being tossed up high into the tree's branches. "Go on, Kiera! Go!" Joe's winded voice trailed off into the distance, as the tree's dark wood consumed him.

"Joe! Joe!" Kiera screamed. The surrounding silence was deafening. "Joe?"

No response. The wooden hands that stole her friend had turned to rotten trees once again. Kiera ran on, her legs seeming to take over. Weaving through the remaining trees, one by one they reached for her. One by one, each failed, turning back into their former shapes. She skidded ungracefully to the path's end, panting.

"Joe!" she cried, mortified, her cries bouncing off the eerie silence. Her heart told her Joe was gone. Wishing now she'd told her Uncle Tom. He'd know what to do, he always did.

Kiera sank down rocking herself, sobbing. *Not Joe, Not him.* In the distance she heard a familiar barking. It was Terrence scampering toward her. He ran through the pathway of trees that now remained motionless, as if the little dog was no threat. Still, Kiera couldn't be sure. "Run, Terrence! Come on, boy, come on!" Terrence leapt into her arms. She clutched him tightly, sobbing into his scruffy fur. "Where've you been, boy? I thought I'd lost you, too." For a moment, she wasn't completely alone, until her quest beckoned once again.

"She's here! It's so exciting. In a few short moments, I will be everlasting, the ruler of this world. Then, I will conquer all worlds and reign over the entire universe!" The Witch Queen cackled at her own wretched brilliance.

"Secure your posts but let the girl think she has the upper hand. Hide yourselves until I give the signal." Her disfigured entourage melted back into the walls, camouflaging their huge stone bodies.

* * * *

Kiera stood at the mouth of the dark palace, hesitating. Terrence was silent for once. He looked up at her as if awaiting orders. Kiera squeezed Zakk tightly and hoped that somewhere inside the doll, the boy was still alive.

"If only Maddy were here. How wrong could I have been?" Kiera closed her eyes and concentrated. "Joe, if you can hear me, I'll find you, I promise." Swallowing hard, opening her eyes, feeling isolated. The only thing to do was finish what she'd started and try and keep all her promises. Without a plan, except maybe to beg for Zakk's life.

The great doors before her swung open slowly. Cold air and the putrid smell of death hit her senses from inside. Without thinking, her foot sprang forward and stepped over the entrance.

"Err, hello." The tomb-like cave echoed her words. Kiera circled, studying her surroundings. In front, a pathway led to a darkened room ahead. To one side stood a pair of tall iron doors that made her quiver, which made no sense. Kiera sneaked quickly past them, shushing Terrence as they went.

"Ah, at last. I've been waiting for you for so long." The monotone voice greeted her in the doorway. "Come closer, my dear. It's rude to enter a person's house and not introduce one's self." Kiera slowly moved forward, like she'd flown from her body, and all she could do was watch. "Lights," clapped the Witch Queen. A dim blue highlighted their female forms. Kiera gasped, recognizing the woman's cold eyes, now framed by sharp, ghastly features. The Witch Queen smirked.

"The one I've been searching for is here, after all these years. The girl that legend foretold would save Zantar."

Kiera puzzled; she could have sworn she saw a passing fear in those dead eyes.

"You've got the wrong girl…" she gulped.

"Come closer, my child. I have a gift for you." Pointing a lank finger toward the corner of the cave. Kiera was horrified by the sight of Daz hanging from his feet. Blood dripped down his clawed, lifeless body. Kiera looked down to what seemed to be a large hole in the floor beneath him.

"I—I don't understand."

"Well now, it's simple. That, my dear, is the Pit of Eternity. Your body never quite hits the bottom. You sink fathoms deep, into your own plague of nightmares. Poor chap never quite knew where his loyalties lay. Now you can decide where yours are."

"What?" Kiera gasped.

"It's your little friend 'Daz,' or that lovely ring on your finger, and of course, I'd like my prince back. Which is it to be?"

Googe stepped from the shadows.

"My Queen, it'sss nearly time. It'sss almossst sseven o'clock."

"Come on, girly," the Witch Queen snapped. "Time is tick-tocking, tick-tocking." Kiera looked from the ring to Daz and back again. "Do you choose a long and loyal friend, who despite knowing your true identity, risked his life and more to protect you? Or a prince you've only known a short time and will very soon be just a child's plaything. It's a simple choice." The queen's voice became shriller, trying to hurry Kiera's decision.

"I-I-I." Kiera simply couldn't decide who would live or die. The Witch Queen was right on the facts but so wrong about how she felt for Zakk. She'd always known Zakk, even before she'd met him. Fate tied them together from their earliest dreams. He was the missing puzzle piece. Kiera couldn't face a future without him.

"This may help you decide." The witch threw a goblet of wine; the liquid hit the air, freezing like glass creating a mirror into another realm. "Take a good look, my dear." Kiera peered into it. Patterns swirled. Everything seemed a little cloudy at first. Kiera's heart pounded witnessing Joe being slowly chewed and digested inside a tree's gut. Sliding down and down, whimpering in pain, his tortured expression swirled into a grey mass. "Keep watching!" Kiera peered in closer, out of the smoky shapes came the image of Maddy. Two huge wolf-like creatures set upon her friend, their teeth sliding into her like butter. Kiera felt nauseas.

"No! Stop it. Stop, I can't take anymore." Kiera sank to the ground. "Are my friends dead?"

"No. But they soon will be if you choose your prince. This is what will happen. Only you can change it." The Witch Queen leaned forward on her thrown in anticipation. "Choose quickly, dear."

Kiera's hands trembled taking Zakk from inside her coat, holding the toy out to the witch.

"I'm so sorry, Zakk," she whispered, taking a few steps nearer to the grinning enemy. "I can't do this."

Chapter Twenty-One

The Witch Queen stretched out a hand, eager to take the doll.

"Well done. I knew you had a brain somewhere behind those pretty eyes."

Kiera shakily raised the silent prince toward the brittle hand. A whooshing sound passed by as Terrence flew, knocking the doll to the ground. Zakk awoke with a sharp thud. The Witch Queen stood up, looking flustered.

"Ouch! What the—?" Kiera dove like a rugby player, reaching Zakk first.

"Glad you're back," she whispered to him, rolling out of on-coming danger.

"What's happening?" Zakk asked.

"No time. We haven't won yet."

"Have you still got the ring?"

Kiera flashed her hand, showing it glistening on her finger.

"You need to get my father's ring from her, too. Get it!" Zakk pleaded.

Kiera rose up, but Terrence was already on the case. Leaping high through the air, knocking the Witch Queen off her feet. She tried desperately to wrestle him off.

"Googe! Help me at once!" Googe stepped back into the shadows. "Googe, you imbecile! Where are you?" The witch sounded oddly vulnerable, for one so powerful. Kiera ran to the dog's aid, sitting on the woman's chest, prising the ring from her spindly finger.

"Guards! Guards," the queen pathetically yelled.

The gigantic rock creatures unfolded themselves from the walls and shunted forward, heading straight for Kiera and the brave little dog.

Terrence yapped repeatedly in front of Kiera, as if to protect her. Kiera frantically tried to find a gap between the approaching terrors, but to no avail. They were now shoulder to shoulder, a solid circle of rock giants holding her inside.

"Quick, Kiera, put on the ring! The two rings together are more powerful than any evil she possesses." Zakk bellowed.

Kiera did so, and a fusion of coloured lights and a familiar tune, rang out around the palace. The tune must have been some sort of high-pitched torture to the queen's guards. They froze, then exploded, catapulting them into thousands of rock pieces. Kiera shielded her eyes from the debris. Both rings stopped emitting their high-pitched humming, a woman's soft voice sang out in its place. Then sound and lights faded.

"That was my mother's voice," Zakk whispered. "How is that possible?"

"We'll look for answers later. Right now, I've got to help Daz." Kiera ran toward the pit. A huge force knocked her to the ground. Blackness overhead swallowed her up as Albatron flew at Daz, biting at his binds with its sharp iron beak. The ropes began to fray.

"I may have lost the ring, but I still have death at my disposal." The Witch Queen laughed with relish.

Kiera reached out a hand to grab for him. When Daz began to fall, it was like watching a horror movie that wouldn't end. She didn't even notice the crazed yapping of her faithful little friend. Leaning further over, thinking if she could just get a hand to him, maybe she could hold on long enough to stop him falling.

"Yes! Gotcha!" Kiera caught his foot and was clinging on tighter than her muscles could endure. Daz opened his eyes slightly and looked up at her upside-down face.

"Kiera?"

Kiera was shoved hard from behind.

"Oh no you don't, little misssy!" Googe hissed with venom, as the two friends were launched further over the side. The pit's stomach rumbled in anticipation of its next feed.

"Googe, you fool! The rings!" The Witch Queen screamed.

"No, Your Highnesss. No ringsss, no threat! You will sstill rule. No one hasss to know you lossst them."

"Good point." Raising a cunning brow. Her sidekick may be promoted yet.

Chapter Twenty-Two

Kiera held onto the pit's edge for dear life. It was almost too much to hold herself up as well as Daz. Still gripping tightly onto his ankle, her nails digging into his flesh as the weight of him pulled them deeper down the vacuous hole.

"Let me go, Kiera, it's my time. I won't take you with me."

Kiera let out an almighty groan.

"I will not let you die, Daz Firth. Do you hear?" Kiera's muscles spasmed, gritting her teeth, trying to ride over the pain.

"Kiera, what does your heart tell you?" Daz's voice calmed. His eyes welled with tears.

"That I'm alone." Kiera refused to listen to the nagging thoughts whispering that she was about to lose another friend.

"You are never alone. It just feels that way. Save your strength. Save yourself. Time is running out for this world. You have to let me go." Daz pleaded.

She could hear Zakk close by, telling her to be strong. To be the girl he knew she was. A new determination pumped within. The rings on her finger shone so brightly, that a fresh burst of energy surged through her body. Were the rings responsible or was it her sole determination?

"Nooo!" she bellowed. The rings on her finger pulsated, illuminating the pit walls around them. Feeling as strong as an Amazonian warrior, she began to swing Daz underneath, like a trapeze act, until he too could grab the pit wall. She panted.

"Wow, Kiera! How the hell did you manage to— never mind." Daz held on. "I'm gonna try and push you up. Take it steady. Don't look down!" Climbing toward her, he began nudging her upward. Every inch they advanced felt like a mile of torture. Pushing, with all the strength he could gather from his tired body, until Kiera slumped over the top and out of the pit's hungry mouth. She lay face down for a few seconds. There was movement at her side.

"Oh, Daz, I—" She turned her face, expecting Daz to be there. Instead, a pair of long pointy boots. She raised her head to see who owned them.

"Hello again." The Witch Queen cocked her head to one side, smirking. "You two make quite thrilling entertainment. Pity it must come to an end. Oh, and look, here comes your little stalker now, behind you as always. Say bye-bye!"

With that, the witch drew up a heel, stamping down hard on Daz's fingers as he reached over the edge. Kiera squealed as Daz cascaded downward, flinging herself to the hole's lip.

"Daz!"

"Save my sister, Kier- -aaa..." His voice trailed off, body plummeting into the darkness.

Kiera crashed onto the ground. She couldn't bring herself to move. Trying to think of home and Uncle Tom's arms around her where she would be safe. Opening her eyes, wishing to be back in her room, but upon seeing this dead new world, she unleashed a moan from the root of her being. Rage screamed from her gut like a siren.

"No more." Slowly standing, feeling like a walking bruise. "No more!" she boomed at the Witch Queen. An electric pulse of light shot from both rings on her finger, throwing Kiera backward, off her feet.

The Witch Queen's face fell in disbelief. Kiera was dazed, but the rings didn't stop. The rainbow of light spun toward her enemy, cuffing her wrists and ankles. The witch shrieked and wailed. Kiera's finger rose upward, tilting her rival into the air. As if angry, the binds of pure light became fire. Pulling the Witch Queen's wrists and ankles, in a slow tug-of-war that she couldn't possibly win. Tighter and harder, they pulled. Stretching her out as if she were made of dough.

Kiera watched wide-eyed as the witch writhed in excruciating agony. The four straps of fire ate at her skin, like she may be ripped in half at any moment.

"Stop!" the Witch Queen pleaded, almost looking human for a second.

What am I doing? How could she let these dark thoughts consume her? Kiera lowered her finger. Both rings dulled. The fiery binds unravelled; the witch plummeted toward the hard floor. Kiera turned away. Nothing. No sound. No crash of the witch's skinny body on impact. Kiera turned in confusion. Albatron had caught the burnt, frail body of her enemy, swooping low, flying out of the large open doorway. Kiera watched the metal bird, until it became a tiny dot on the skyline.

All was silent.

"Kiera?" A faint voice called from the darkness. Kiera snapped back to reality, remembering the mission wasn't over yet. She scampered around the floor.

"Zakk. Zakk! Where are you?"

"I'm here." Kiera's skin iced. The little doll hung over the Pit of Eternity, held by the scaly hand of Googe.

"Nice try, Misssy! But you forgot one ssmall thing. Me!" Terrence barked wildly and raced at Googe. Googe dropped Zakk down into the nothingness. "Ssweet dreamsss, little Prince."

"No, Zakk!" Kiera threw herself over the edge of the pit without thought, because if he died, so would she.

Chapter Twenty-Three

The clock struck seven.

"And now for our final act of the evening, Miss Kiera Matthews!" The spotlight shone into Kiera's face. Madam Swift began to play 'Somewhere Over the Rainbow', on the piano. Kiera stood motionless, trying to get her bearings. Looking down, expecting to see her bruised and bloody body. Instead, she wore a white floaty dress that Maddy helped her pick out last month. What new test was this? Was it the pit's torment? Was she still falling? Where was Zakk? She didn't have time to be in this place. *Wake up*, she told herself. *Wake up!*

The intro of the song played, three times at least, until Madam Swift became concerned and her sausage-like fingers stopped.

"Are you okay, Miss Matthews?" she barked, in a baritone voice.

"Sing Kiera, sing," a voice from the wings whispered. Kiera turned to see Maddy looking worried. Kiera closed her eyes. *I have no right to sing. I lost. I can't sing now.* The mumblings of the audience washed over her as parents, and teachers alike, became uncomfortable with the awkward girl before them. Kiera glanced at the rings on her finger and heard that familiar tune in her mind. Feeling stronger now with fresh warmth on her skin. Imagining Joe and Daz, smiling at her, urging her on. She could hear Zakk's voice speaking softly into her ear, encouraging her. If this was an endless dream, at least he was in it.

Her eyes flew open. The thumping of her heart was deafening. A beautiful sound escaped her lips. A song she didn't know but recognised. Somehow, she was here singing it. The onlookers watched silently, taking in the song. The words formed a lullaby. Kiera pictured a gentle blonde woman, rocking a baby forward and back. Moonlight eclipsed the soft beauty of the woman's face. The audience seemed captivated, enchanted by the young songbird. Kiera reached the end of the sweet song. Feeling great sadness, yet strangely comforted. She had lost many loved ones this day. How could she ever be the same again?

The crowd paused. Uncle Tom shot to his feet, brimming with pride, clapping wildly. The rest of the spectators followed his lead, a few shouting for more. Kiera was immune to their praise, still unsure if this was real. Maddy ran onto the stage.

"You've won, Kiera!"

"No, Maddy. I lost." Looking into her friend's eyes, letting the tears finally escape.

Chapter Twenty-Four

Kiera sat alone, letting both feet dangle over the edge of the pier. Staring vacantly out to the horizon, trying to think of the positive things still left in her life. Her Uncle Tom, who thankfully hadn't disappeared and still seemed to love her no matter what. School holidays were over tomorrow, and she'd barely said two words to him. The police questioned her on numerous occasions about the disappearance of Daz Firth and Joe Crosby. But any mention of them, Kiera became inaudible and erupted with tears. She'd failed them. The only person she had really spoken to was Maddy. She had to tell her best friend the truth. She owed her that. Maddy grieved for Daz every minute of every waking day.

Kiera's guilt for her lost friends ate away at her. She'd get through a shift at 'Tom's Cabin' and then perch at the end of the pier to watch the sunset, wishing Zakk had chosen somebody else. Somebody stronger. Wishing more than anything else, that she'd see her three friends gliding up the prom toward her. They would laugh and joke, like they always did. But no one came. She watched the tide swish in and out, like it too wanted to be her friend, and then left again when it realised what she'd done.

"Hey," a soft voice from behind.

"Maddy!" Kiera jumped to her feet, grabbing her tightly. "I'm so glad to see you. How you holding up?"

"I'm getting there," Maddy lied through her smile.

"I thought you blamed me."

"No, of course I don't, silly. Can't imagine what you've gone through... are going through. But us doing it alone, can't be good," Maddy sighed.

"I've missed you so much, Maddy." Kiera flung her arms around her friend once again, feeling some of the stress slowly floating away. "I just want them back," she cried.

"Me too...me too...Err, who's that?" Maddy whispered, peering over Kiera's shoulder. "Is it her, Kiera? Has she come for you?" Maddy trembled. Kiera slowly pivoted. A dark, hooded figure walked toward them. Its heavy footsteps a deadly countdown as it walked the wooded slats of the long pier. Kiera sucked in a breath, in anticipation. "Is it her, Kiera?" Maddy gasped, edging backward to the end of the pier, so close to the sea below.

The figure's face emerged from the shadow of the hood. A tall boy with piercing green eyes. Curly golden locks danced lightly around his face in the sea breeze. Standing tall before them, both girls were mesmerized.

"Hello, Kiera." She looked hard at this stranger, knowing deep down, that he wasn't so strange after all. "You did it, Kiera, you saved me."

"Zakk?" She knew his voice. No one else made her feel so calm and safe.

"Yes, it's me," he nodded. Kiera jumped into his arms like a frightened child.

"It's good to see you too," Zakk said, closing his eyes and stroking her hair.

"But how? You fell. You fell..."

"You're right, I did fall. But with your strength combined with the ring's powers, it was too great a force for any evil to fight. On the stroke of seven, I found myself back in my bed, and I was 'me' again. Don't you see? Your surge of love, and determination, happened exactly on my birthday, seven o' clock. So, you did it with no time to spare. Plus, you had both rings...It's like my parents joining together to protect me in some way…" Zakk grabbed her arms. "Look, we must act quickly if you want to save your friend."

"He's still alive?" Kiera's heart raced faster than her thoughts.

"Yes, and we have to go now."

Maddy stepped forward. "Take me too, I want to help."

"Alas, I cannot. This is Kiera's quest alone," Zakk replied.

"But why? Why is it mine alone?" Kiera frowned.

"All truths will reveal themselves to us in time. But now there is no time. Trust me once again. You didn't let me down, and I won't abandon you." Zakk squeezed her shoulder.

"Please, Maddy stay here, where I know you're safe. That'll be all the help I need."

Kiera hugged her disappointed friend. "I'll be back soon. If anything happens…if anything happens to me, tell my uncle I love him."

"Kiera, take my hand." Zakk said.

Kiera took a deep breath and put her hand in his.

SACRIFICES

Chapter One

"Wake up!"

His eyes opened wide, lashes beating fiercely against a new violent brightness. Trying to gauge his surroundings, searching his mind for a single clue, a memory that might lead to how he came to be here. The unfamiliarity of both brought about panic. Stretching out his limbs, attempting to sit up. A searing pain sent a jolt to every body part and he recoiled like a defensive snake. Mind and body collapsed in unison as his limbs dangled down like paper lanterns. The image of a girl jumped before his streaming lids, and a faint smile caressed his mouth.

Time danced in and out; first a Quickstep then a Waltz. Images too dark for his mind flicked randomly. Then the nothingness came and took root in his soul, drenching him in emptiness with no sense of haste. This was the sloth, the torment.

The cycle would start over, and his mind slowly made sense of them now. Old memories confused with scenes of war and pain. People he loved hurting; people he loved attacking him! Had this happened? Was this how they'd left him?

As his brain tricked him with unbearable ideas, tears pinched away at his eyes. The name, 'Kiera' escaped his lips.

"Open your eyesss; open your eyesss! I command you, sslave, open your eyesss!"

Joe's eyes flickered in horror in reaction to the venomous tone.

"Ah, at lasst! Felt like joining uss, did we?"

"Where…" Joe's voice broke with dryness. It felt like weeks since he last drank. "Where… where am I? What are you doing to me?" A beautiful face sprang into his thoughts, and the haze began to lift. "Where is Kiera? Where is she?" he feebly demanded. Joe tried to sit up, but the tight binds pulled him back down to the slab that held him fast.

"Googe," a weak voice quivered from somewhere behind. "The boy's not ready. Fire up the machine and blast him again."

From above, two metal stalks with blue neon lights at their ends swung rapidly toward him, wrapping around his forehead. Flashing their brightness directly into his vision. A small, rodent-like squeal vibrated around his skull. Silence fell again as Joe started to slip into the nightmare, which for now was more welcoming than reality.

"The boy iss sstronger than we expected, Your Majessty."

"Maybe," her frail voice drifted from behind the curtain. "Or maybe his feelings for *her* are stronger than we realised. Interesting, we can use this to our advantage. Crank up the voltage. Let's turn all that sickening love into beautiful heart-pumping hate!"

Joe's unconscious body contorted in pure agony, and the frail voice sighed with pleasure.

Chapter Two

"And who is *she*?" Kiera blurted most unattractively.

"Kiera, let me introduce you to Jude."

Zakk smiled, patting Jude lightly on the shoulder. The small girl changed from porcelain white to lobster red at his touch. Kiera felt a little pushed out. Perhaps a little jealous of this mousey blonde, who was actually a little plain. Her features were a tad too small for her round face, and her naturally turned down mouth gave the impression of a constant frown.

"Jude is an important ally. She's our eyes and ears. Our connection to the rebellion, working inside the Dark Palace. I would *really* like it if you two could get along."

He strolled over to Kiera, lightly manoeuvring her until she was toe to toe with this *new rival*. After eyeballing one another for a few moments, Kiera stepped back, offering her hand.

"I guess it's nice to meet you." She would hold judgement for now, but this *newbie* almost felt like a replacement.

Jude's face lit up in gratitude. When she smiled, it was like looking at a different girl, an almost attractive one. Kiera began to unlike her again.

"This is the only entrance left to the palace, all the others have been magically locked," Jude informed them.

"Why has this one been overlooked?" Kiera fidgeted. Zakk made a strange spluttering sound.

"This is the sewer tunnel." He sighed. "The Witch Queen probably thinks nobody would be crazy enough to attempt passage this way."

"Plus," continued Jude, "it's really cramped, so it does take a while, not so much for me." Jude laughed. "I'm quite unique in size." It was true—from behind Jude could have been mistaken for a young child. "It's a family thing. I think it kinda makes me endearing." She shrugged.

Zakk messed her hair affectionately and Kiera raised an untrusting eyebrow.

"Well, I'm not going in there," Kiera huffed, crossing her arms like a defiant four-year-old.

"Why not?" Zakk's asked.

"For starters, how long exactly is that tunnel? I mean, the palace looks tiny from here."

"If I can do it, you can," Jude said, a bit too cocky for Kiera's liking.

"And…and if the smell is anything to go by…" Kiera grimaced. "Then err…no thanks."

"I don't understand. You and I have faced far worse than this, and yet you're frightened of a tiny tunnel? Come on, Matthews! You want to go first?"

"I've already told you, Zakk, I am not going in there. Not even for you."

Kiera cringed upon hearing herself. The three stood silently for a few awkward minutes.

"I don't like confined spaces. Okay, I said it." Kiera half whispered.

"Look," said Zakk holding her shoulders. "Do you want to save your friend?"

"Yes, of course, you know I do…more than anything." Wiping several tears with her sleeve.

"I'm going in. If you don't follow, then this could be goodbye—forever." Zakk lightly kissed her forehead. He turned, dropped to the ground, and disappeared into the forbidding tunnel. "For-ev-er!" Zakk shouted behind.

"I'll go next then," Jude said, getting into position.

"Err, no. I'll go next." Kiera pushed in front to the entrance. "If I go last, I may not go at all." *And I don't want you anywhere near my Zakk*, she thought as she smiled sweetly at a disgruntled Jude.

Kiera tied the chocolate tendrils back off her face and knelt in the entrance. Putting her head inside the hole, the overwhelming stench of faeces stung her eyes.

"Oh God! Oh God!" Wincing, she took the longest breath possible and pictured Joe.

She seemed to have only moved a few inches when it happened. An unfamiliar screech like when you accidentally stand on a cat's paw, escaped Kiera's lungs.

"Eeeeeiiowwww!" Panic took over, feeling like she had expanded in the tight space. Like a bottled cork, she was completely wedged.

"Sshhh! Kiera, what's wrong?" Zakk asked.

"I think she's stuck." Jude's muffled words rumbled from behind.

"How can you be? I'm bigger than both of you, and I made it through—just." Zakk slowly reversed, edging closer to Kiera. Jude continued forward.

"I can't breathe! I can't breathe!"

Kiera wriggled frantically, trying to escape the tiny area. The three of them were altogether now in a compact line, bottom to nose—bottom to nose.

"Kiera, listen to me," Zakk said, as he quarter-turned his head.

"I can't move, Zakk. I can't do this!"

"Kiera!" he commanded, sounding almost like the king he would become. "Breathe, just breathe. Sshhh, that's it...calm down. Breathe in and out...in and out…"

Kiera stopped moving and focused on his voice.

"You are not stuck. You just need to tilt your shoulders to the right slightly. On the count of three. One...two...three...tilt!"

"I can't do this," she sobbed.

"You *can* do this; you just need to tilt!" Zakk huffed. "Look," he said, changing his tone. "The smell and dampness isn't one of my best life experiences, but it beats being a doll, any day."

"No…I mean, I can't do this with you anymore. I'm just a girl who likes normal things. Shopping, dancing, singing, hearing the rain against my window at night and…just normal stuff. All this has to be a mistake. Pick someone else."

"Kiera," Zakk whispered. "It's always been you. There can be no-one else."

Kiera heard Jude 'tut' from behind and found herself smiling a little. "We were meant to meet, and you are meant to…" Zakk's words were submerged by the sudden sweet lullaby that emitted from Kiera's ring.

"My mother's voice again. I miss her so much. This is a sign, surely?" With that, Kiera tilted her body and thrust herself onward.

"See! I knew she wasn't really stuck. Drama queen," Jude mumbled.

Zakk snapped back into the moment as the ring's light dimmed, and the sweet tune quietened.

"Come on girls; we have a mission to complete."

"Plus, the fact," Kiera said, "it stinks of cat sick and cheesy feet down here. The rancidness must be singeing your nostril hairs, Zakk."

"Okay, okay. Good to have the old Kiera back. On with the plan— time to move forward."

Chapter Four

The entire assembly hall rippled with rumours and accusations. The students of Stanforth High were suspicious and scared. Some were still embarrassed by the fact that their mother, father, or older sibling had insisted on chaperoning them to school. Most mourned the loss of Joe, the school's star athlete. Some missed the moody gothic boy who would strum his guitar in the dinner hall on a wet day. Everyone wished the two missing boys would just appear, and it had all been part of some crazy schoolboy hoax. Some knew better. Maddy, for one, knew she would never again hear the annoying strumming of Daz's guitar. How she missed those 'noises' now. Hearts were breaking all over this shell-shocked school today.

Now, something new was taking place. It was the first day of term, and Maddy knew this wasn't going to be the usual welcome back speech. Two police officers stood in conference with Mrs. Jackson, (the weebly-wobbly school Head) at the front of the room. The crowd grew silent, almost holding their breath en masse, trying to hear the murmurings of the three secretive stooges.

A sense of fear trembled through the students. Words such as 'death,' 'missing,' and 'boys' carried backward from row to row, until the whispering turned into an unbearable buzzing. Everyone was under suspicion. 'Ferrety-Thirtle' the science teacher, adjusted his tie as his beady eyes shifted, like each student was guilty.

"Can I have everyone's attention please," Mrs. Jackson boomed over the restless crowd. For someone so small, she had some large pipes on her. Chloe and Ben Wilson, the tiresome twins shushed everybody mockingly, trying as usual to catch brownie points.

Everyone fell silent. Maddy braced herself. Had they found her best friend? Was she…?

"Hello, children. My name is Officer Millar," announced the tall, bulbous-nosed gentleman. "This here is Officer Cole." The short, piggy-eyed sidekick nodded in a half grunt. "As you all know, the search for the missing boys is still ongoing." By this, Maddy knew they meant 'at a standstill.' "Anyone with any new information, please come and see myself, or Officer Cole, after this assembly." He coughed dryly.

Maddy gasped as the throat clearing was sure to make way for more bad news. Could all of her friends have been taken by this new evil? Was Kiera okay? What could this double act possibly know? Maddy leaned forward in anticipation.

"Now," said Officer Millar wiping his sweaty forehead. "I am very sorry to tell you another child has been reported missing." The students frantically looked around, trying to gauge who was absent. Maddy stared blankly straight ahead. "Kiera Matthews was last seen leaving home around fifteen forty-five yesterday, heading for a walk along the beach. If anyone has any further information, it is crucial that you come forward." Officer Millar scanned the crowd in misguided hope.

Ben Wilson's arm shot up in the air.

"Is this a murder investigation, Officer Millar?"

"Shut up, Ben, you div!" Chloe pulled his arm down and looked embarrassed at her sniggering brother. Maddy glanced at Chloe, a little unnerved, as this was unusual behaviour for her. For a moment, their eyes locked, and they shared a look between them that said so much.

"Maddison Smith, you will remain behind please." Mrs. Jackson nodded.

All eyes were on Maddy and her cheeks flushed in awkward dread. Did they think she knew more than she was saying? Did they think she was guilty? Did they think she was next?

"See, we made it!" Zakk held a hand out to assist Kiera as she flopped from the sewer hole like a damp squid. Splat!

"Brilliant, more grime." She lay motionless, panting, imitating a thirsty Labrador.

"On your feet, soldier." Zakk laughed fondly, grabbing both arms and pulling her upright.

Kiera quickly assessed their new surroundings. Much to her dismay, they were anything but inviting. However, they were slightly less cramped than the previous sewer crawl. This was just a larger version, slab walls with various mutations of slime breeding. Mass families of fungi webbed across every surface.

"Yikes." Jude clambered out behind them. Zakk gallantly moved into position to catch her. "It's okay; I can do it. I *am* the expert when it comes to tunnels. They don't call me 'mouse' for nothing." Jude blushed as if she didn't quite believe her own hype.

"Okay, expert, is there a towel or something we can use to get all this stuff off our hands?" Kiera held both hands out as far away from herself as possible.

"There are supplies waiting for us. Gosh, Kiera, it's just a bit of poo." Mouse shook her head and laughed. "Just don't put it near your mouth."

"Where to? Oh Leader!" Zakk asked, quickly glancing around.

This new area was just as unpleasant as the tunnel. Not physically perhaps but mentally. Zakk and Kiera both knew it was going to be worse than they could've ever imagined.

"Follow me." Mouse started to scurry away. "The smell gets better, I promise."

Kiera sighed. She should be in class right now, probably listening to 'Ferrety-Thirtle' talking about compounds and stuff. Instead, she was here, down a dark, putrid tunnel that led to…well, possible death.

"At least we can stand up now," Zakk whispered, as always, trying to put a good spin on things.

Jude/Mouse led them on through more damp caves and tunnels.

"Why do we seem to be sloping?" Kiera asked.

"Because we are going down under the palace itself, underground, right, Mouse?"

Mouse nodded, leading them further down as the stone walls dripped gunk onto their skin. They reached a large overhang.

"Stop!" Mouse half-whispered, half-spat, putting her arms out for sheer dramatic effect. "The pathway ends here. You may be shaken by what you are about to witness. Under no circumstances must we be detected." Zakk and Kiera nodded in wide-eyed agreement. "And guys…Oh I mean, Your Majesty." Mouse blushed as she caught his eye. "Try not to fall over the edge."

Dropping to their knees and crawling forward until they ran out of ground. Six eyes looked down. Kiera let out a Chihuahua-like yelp. Zakk shoved his hand over her mouth.

"I hadn't realised how bad things had gotten," Zakk whispered.

Kiera watched as a single tear slid from her chin, all the way down to the ground, hitting the horrific scene below. She hadn't even realised she'd been crying.

Chapter Six

"Err…hello?" Maddy knocked tentatively and peered around 'The Weeble's' office door. An uneasy looking Mrs. Jackson sat behind the desk. Officers Cole and Millar stood at either side, like two bookends. Not the matching kind, maybe the type where one is the cat's upper body and face and the other is the cat's bottom.

"Please, take a seat, Maddison." Mrs. Jackson seemed ruffled, and little beads of sweat formed along her frizzy hairline.

"Okay," Maddison replied, pressing her lips together feeling like a wanted fugitive.

"You are not in any trouble, my dear. This is *not* an interrogation." The Weeble smiled warmly. Maddy glanced quickly to the suspecting eyes of the two officers, gulping in anticipation.

"It's okay, Maddison." A familiar, warmer voice came from behind.

Turning to see Kiera's uncle hovering in the corner. Relaxing instantly, letting out the breath she unknowingly held.

"Now then, Miss." Officer Millar bent down, putting both palms on the pristinely tidy desk. "We know little, but what we do know is *you* were also seen near the pier at around sixteen hundred hours yesterday. Coincidence? I think not." Officer Cole's eyes narrowed behind his partner. What were they accusing her of?

"You're scaring the poor kid." Tom entered, placing his hand on Maddy's shoulder, giving her the 'it'll be alright' squeeze. "Did you see Kiera, Maddy?"

"Err…I did, but only for a minute or two. I had to be back for dinner."

"And what about Miss Matthews?" Officer Cole stepped forward seeming surprised at breaking his own silence.

"Err, err, she, she said she had to think about some stuff. So, I…I…left her."

Officer Millar started pacing. "Did she say anything else? Did you see anyone else? Think…anything that might give us a clue as to the whereabouts of your *friend*."

Maddy cringed at the way he said 'friend,' like he was implying she was less than that, or she was behind all of this. Maddy wanted to jump up and protest her innocence. She wanted to blurt out the bizarre happenings. Since Kiera had found that strange doll, everything had changed. How important it all was, and how unimportant it made her feel. Imagining all the anguish and pain lifting from her tense body, along with all the secrets she promised to hold. But she didn't tell; she couldn't. Deep down, Maddy believed Kiera would come back. She had only been in Zakk's presence briefly, but something about him completely calmed her. He would protect Kiera. She just knew it. So, saying nothing and feeling dumb, as hard questions were fired her way. Weaving and dodging them clumsily; keeping the 'I just don't know,' look on her face.

"Would you mind if I had a moment alone with her, officers, Mrs. Jackson?" Tom smiled charismatically, pushed his glasses up his nose and nodded with authority.

Thank God for Tom, Maddy thought and relaxed back in the chair.

"Hmmm, two minutes," snapped Officer Millar. They left the room and Tom listened at the door until their footsteps went away.

"Right, Maddison!" Tom folded his arms.

"Y-yes?"

"I need to know exactly what Zakk said to Kiera last night before they disappeared, and I need to know right now."

Maddy sprang forward sending the chair backward. "Err…What?"

Chapter Seven

"Well now, what do we have here? Three stowaways?"

The three companions whirled round in unison as Kiera sucked in a breath. Was the game over? Had they been discovered by… Oh, thought Kiera with relief—a scruffy-looking girl. The girl stood confidently, almost arrogantly, before them, hands on hips, surveying them. Who did this ruffian think she was standing before a prince like she owned the world? With her self-cut spiky hair and torn clothes. Under all the dirt, her topaz eyes flickered familiarly, and (with a little conditioner) her hair was almost black. Kiera's gaze continued to float over this newcomer. On assessment, she concluded that together they could take her.

"Mouse, aren't you going to introduce me to your new friends?"

"Oh yes, sorry, Alex." Mouse gestured to them. "This is Prince Za…"

"Of course, I know who he is," Alex teased. "Zakk, right? And you –" Alex turned, looking at Kiera. "You must be the infamous, Kiera. Come to save us all have you? About time I say."

Mouse grimaced. "She doesn't mean it, honest, it's just that, well, things are tough down here."

Kiera nodded; having already seen the scene below, shuddering at the thought of spending one second in it.

"Well, let's get to business." Alex rapidly began firing out information. "The guards' change is nearly over, so I'll have to go back before they notice I'm gone. You three will hide up here until the next change in two hours."

"What's the plan?" Zakk asked, seemingly impressed with Alex.

Kiera noticed a difference in Zakk that made her uneasy. Was he acting… coy? Or was it that he wasn't used to taking orders? She couldn't quite put her finger on it. Kiera and Mouse looked from Zakk to Alex as Zakk shuffled lightly from foot to foot. Did he like her? No, he couldn't... could he? Kiera manoeuvred herself between the two, trying to block Zakk's view. Mouse cleared her throat, pretending to busy herself with her rucksack.

"Right, so what's the plan?" Kiera asked, taking charge of the situation.

Alex seemed unaware, or totally uninterested in the heated feelings ping-ponging about the frozen cave. Alex rifled off more instructions.

"Guards change at 08:00; this takes roughly five minutes. In this time, you will come down this mineshaft and take one prisoner each. No more, no less. This will go on every two hours until I have all of my team, of which there are nine. One each as we cannot risk detection." Alex took a breath, allowing time for them to absorb the information. "Once you have them, direct them back up the sewer tunnel where they will wait for the others to join them. Once you have all nine, take them to the safety of your kingdom."

"Err...Alex." Zakk seemed hesitant on butting in while the girl was in full flow. "One question, isn't my palace being guarded by the witch's men?"

"That's the strange thing. We thought she would've moved in by now. For some reason, she seems to detest the place. No guards, no patrols. It's just left kind of barren, since you... When it's safe for me to leave, I will join you. Put on the clothes provided." She looked at Kiera's red hoodie and sneaker ensemble. "These will help you blend in. Stay quiet. Stay warm. Stay focused."

With that, Alex threw herself down the mineshaft, dropping out of sight.

"Here's your towel. You two ought to settle and get warm. It's a long time to sit around waiting," Mouse whispered, tossing the dirty rags at them.

Zakk was quiet. Had he heard anything they'd said? Kiera guessed by the faraway look in his eyes and the small cheeky grin, he was thinking about Alex. The three began changing into their ugly attire. The darkness of the cave covered most of their blushes. Zakk in one corner; the girls in another.

"So," Mouse broke the silence that Kiera was rather enjoying. "You into Zakk or what?"

"What?" Kiera laughed, feeling her ears burning in embarrassment.

"Well, you two are pretty close. Are you a couple?"

"No! We're not."

"But you're into him, right?" Mouse narrowed her eyes on Kiera's as if trying to see into her mind.

"No, not right… And may I just say, you're quite rude for someone I just met."

Kiera finished dressing and crossed her arms, positioning her back to the niggling little annoyance. Standing in the darkness for a few moments, Kiera thought about Jude's questions and realised she couldn't answer them. She felt something for Zakk, but what that was she hadn't figured out yet. Then there was Joe. The guy she was bursting to see again, thinking he was dead almost destroyed her. Kiera warmed, smiling at the thought of their reunion.

"We'd best all huddle together in this corner. It seems the driest spot." Mouse beckoned to Zakk.

Kiera turned to Zakk for approval. Looking at him dressed as an urchin, Kiera couldn't help but splutter a laugh.

"I wish I had a camera."

"Sshhh," Mouse hissed, eyebrows joining in the middle.

"Sorry." Kiera bit her lip.

"Okay, okay, let it go." Zakk waved his hand. "The truth is, unless we defeat this evil and bring Zantar back to its former glory, it won't matter what I wear, or who I am."

Kiera nodded. Rags or not, Zakk's presence shone regally, and his beautiful emerald eyes still sparkled with hope.

Chapter Eight

The curtain was pulled across, like it had been for so long now. Googe popped his head around.

"Your Majessty, it iss nearly time for your next treatment. Are you able to sstand, or do you need ssome assissstance?"

The frail, weathered woman pushed herself up slowly from her sickbed and swung her feet over the side. "I can manage, thank you, Googe."

Googe bowed. Having heard this speech every day, he positioned himself for the outcome of her sheer stubbornness.

"Ahhhhhhhh." The defeated screech pierced the palace walls.

Googe sprang with his lizard legs. He timed it just right every time, catching her before her feeble carcass hit the floor. The first time he wasn't as precise and got more than a lashing of her tongue.

"Put me back on the bed for now."

"Yess, Your Highnesss. May I ssuggessst that today we give you four treatmentsss. It painsss me to ssee you like thisss. To ssee what that girl hasss done to you painsss me greatly."

"Fine. Don't go getting all sickly on me please. Four treatments should make me strong again, every hour—on the hour. Go! Bring me the next urchins."

Googe bowed and grovelled, the few hairs on his chin almost touching the floor.

"I already have two candidatesss waiting outssside. I will insstruct your guardsss to catch two more." He backed out of the Witch Queen's chambers, still spouting cringe-worthy compliments to his frail mistress.

A young woman and a pale-faced girl wriggled and squirmed in a zombie guard's grip.

"Bring them in!" The Witch Queen's voice broke with weakness.

"Please, please, Your Highness. Please don't do this. What can we do for you…anything? Keep us working your mines… Let your guards whip and beat us… But please, not this. We've seen the others come out of here…they're different."

The woman clasped her hands in prayer and sank to her knees. The young girl at her side began to whimper.

"Bring them forward for the Queen'sss insspection," Googe ordered the zombie guard.

The girls kicked and pushed their feet hard into the ground but to no avail. They were pushed along like pebbles, arriving just short of the thick velvet curtain.

"Come a little closer, ladies."

The voice played with their fears. The curtain drew back, and the Witch Queen was standing on her own two legs for the first time since the battle with Kiera.

"Your Majesssty," Googe chimed, running to her side. "It'sss ssoo good to ssee you healthier at lassst!"

"Yes, yes, Googey." Waving him aside.

"I have brought you youthful offeringsss thisss time, Your Greatnesss. Their energy sshould feed you well."

"Mmmm." Looking them slowly up and down. "They do look tasty; good work, Googe."

"Alwaysss at your sservice. Alwaysss here to pleassse you."

Yes! Let's get on with it, shall we."

Googe nodded and stepped back to watch. He loved having a front row seat. He loved watching greatness at work.

"Please, I beg you. Please don't!" the pale girl cried out.

"I don't know why you're so sad. You are doing your queen a great favour. You are part of something life-changing, something never-ending—me! I'm only borrowing a little essence. Don't you want to see me well again?" The evil tormentor pouted, like a stubborn child. "You'll get it back eventually. Until that day you will just have a little holiday in your minds, where nothing will matter. It may be quite nice for you really. Better than working in a mine all day long. Of course, you still will be, you just won't know it."

The pair hollered in unison as the witch placed a bony hand on each of their heads and sunk her tawny, crusty nails into their temples. The victims screamed like lobsters being boiled alive. Googe jumped up and down in excitement. Their bodies shook violently. The Witch Queen straightened up and roared in laughter.

"I feel it! The power…the power!" The two girls slumped to their knees, expressionless and mute. "It won't be long now, my Googe, and I will be back leading armies—ruling worlds!"

"Yesss, yesss, My Queen."

"Get them out of here. They are ruining the décor. Bring more, bring more!" The Witch Queen swirled around her bed, as if she was fifteen again.

"At once, My Misstresss."

Chapter Nine

"We'll take it in turns to sit in the middle for the extra warmth. Ladies first." Zakk smiled at Kiera.

"That's me then," Mouse said, diving in-between the two of them.

Zakk shrugged; eyebrows raised. Kiera smiled sweetly back. A few moments passed as they listened to awful grindings down below. Slaves being whipped, forced to work harder. Kiera felt sick, scared.

"Would you stop fidgeting!" Kiera whispered.

"Sorry, I fidget when I'm nervous, and when I'm freezing… Zakk, could you put your arm around me please. I'm so cold." Jude asked.

Kiera blew out her cheeks in resentment when Zakk did as Jude asked.

"Five more minutes, Mouse, and then it's my turn in the middle."

Mouse buried deep into Zakk's shoulder making an 'mmmm' sound. His awkward expression said it all, easing Kiera's mind.

"Right, that's it, Ratty, switch places."

Mouse snarled back and unwillingly gave up her spot. Kiera, now in the middle, felt content next to Zakk, where for some obscure reason, she belonged. For a few relaxed moments, letting her mind empty, resting her cheek to his chest. Feeling safe in his arms as they tightened around her. The thudding of his heartbeat soaked into her, sighing blissfully. Losing herself in the embrace.

* * * *

"So, have you ever-like-been, in love?" Mouse stumbled over the words.

"Err, no I haven't. I'm still very young." Zakk looked everywhere but at Mouse.

The three sat huddled together along the cold, fungus-covered wall. Kiera was asleep in the middle doing a cute little whimper every time she breathed out. Zakk cradled her like she was sacred.

"Of course." Zakk stiffened. "I don't really get time for such pleasures with all my royal duties."

"Of course, of course." Mouse fell silent for a second. "Do you believe in love at first sight?" Mouse whispered, frowning at Zakk's arm fondly placed around the other girl.

"I don't really know." Zakk seemed puzzled at this line of questioning. "I guess you can like someone upon seeing them, and I guess you will just know it." He smiled, but not at Mouse, and she wondered who this secret smile was for.

"But," Mouse stammered. "What would be the point of you even looking? You're born into a world where marriages are arranged from birth."

"Oh no." Zakk chuckled, shaking his blond locks. "My father abolished that law when he fell for my mother. Gosh, Mouse, you really have been in this cave for too long."

"Oh," Mouse muttered, turning her face away into the darkness.

"Ahhhhhh!"

Kiera's head shot up from the warmth of Zakk's chest. Some god-awful noise had ripped her from a dream. The three of them scurried to the overhang and looked down to see what had shaken the slaves so badly. A plumpish woman played tug-of-war with a young boy. However, the guards on his other arm were much stronger.

"That's Eric, one of the King's Guards. What the…? What's wrong with him?" Zakk gasped.

"Shhh," Mouse warned. "The King's Guards work for *her* now. They're under some sort of mind control spell. Sort of zombies to her will. Down there, if you're not zombified, you are a slave, or a victim of essence stealing… soon to be brainless."

"Please! Please! Don't take my boy. Take me instead."

Another burly man stepped forward, who Zakk recognised as being the king's faithful lieutenant.

"We will take you both," he droned, in an emotion-free tone.

The three onlookers gasped in horror as the two prisoners were escorted away. Kiera could still hear the young boy sobbing.

"That's it! I'm going down there." Zakk sprang to his feet. Both girls yanked him down again.

"You cannot ruin the plan now," Mouse snapped. "I'm sorry, Your Majesty, but we must stick to the plan."

"She's right." Kiera placed a hand on his arm. "You know she is."

Chapter Ten

"Say something…say anything. Look, I know this has come as a bit of a shock…" Tom pushed the tortoise-shell glasses up his nose, a nervous habit he didn't realise he had. "Maddison…are you okay?"

Maddy sat silently in the chair looking up at him wide-eyed, mouth gaping. Tom waved his hand in front of her unblinking expression. "Hello? Earth to Maddison! Are you still with me?"

"Who… and, whoa!" Maddy breathed out finally. "This is major! Totally, stupendously major!"

Suddenly, all the questions she had, flooded out.

"How long have you known? Are you really her uncle? Are you one of them? What shall we do now? Are you evil? Why didn't you stop Daz dying?" She lowered her face and tried to shake off the sorrowful anger she felt. "Maybe…" she said, her head still lowered, "you are evil, or you would have helped." Tensing, trying to estimate the probability of getting past him. She may not be Joe in the speed stakes, but she figured Tom to be at least forty.

"It's okay." Tom clasped her chin, gently lifting it.

He bent to her level. Maddy didn't see any darkness in him, just Tom, good old reliable Tom.

"But I don't understand… I…"

"All you need to know right now is yes, I am Kiera's uncle. And no, I am definitely not evil."

Maddison smiled a little at ever thinking such things. Tom grinned back before his expression became quite stern.

"Most importantly…Kiera cannot know about my involvement in this. Nobody can know."

"What?" Maddy shot from the chair. "She's my best friend, are you kidding me!"

Tom took hold of the door handle.

"Come on." Smiling, looking over the top of his glasses. "Let's see if we can bust you out of this joint. Let's take a walk. Go and get your coat, and I'll clear it with Mrs. Jackson."

Tom left the office. His loafers squeaked in the uncomfortably silent corridors. Maddy walked out in a daze, anxiety beating wildly in her chest. Palms sweating at the thought of the unknown.

"So, what was all that about, Smith?"

"Huh?" Maddy jumped.

Leaning against the lockers with her arms folded, draped in designer labels, was Chloe Wilson. There was not a bobbed hair out of place, and expensive make-up had been applied with precision over her accusing face. Apple-green eyes stared deeply into Maddison's, until Maddison couldn't help but look away.

"I said," Chloe spoke slowly. "What was all that about?"

"I...I...that's none of your business, Wilson." Maddy tried to push past the overbearing girl, but Chloe stepped forward, blocking her path.

"You will tell me, Smith, or else!"

"Or else what? What do you care anyway? Want to be the first to spread the gossip, do you?"

Chloe narrowed her eyes, and then her whole face seemed to soften. Maddy didn't recognise *this* girl.

"Okay, so I'm not Kiera's biggest fan, but I don't want her dead or anything. I mean, she's not that bad." Chloe chewed her lip and shrugged.

"Whoa! Don't tell me the great Chloe Wilson actually owns a heart." Putting her hands on her hips. "As I told you, it's none of *your* business. You can't just be a total unfeeling cow, for like eight years, and then pretend you're actually human. Move aside!"

"I don't expect you to…" Chloe's speech was cut short, as her troublesome twin came around the corner bouncing a basketball.

"Hey now, sis, slumming it with the scum today, are we?" Ben Wilson snorted a laugh. "Or should I say, watch your back, Ginger here might do you in. Like she does with all her friends. Who will be next on murderous Maddison's list of death?" Ben dramatically held his throat as if being choked.

A few passers-by chuckled. Many still hadn't yet come to terms with their missing peers and tutted in distaste.

"I was just getting the gossip—right, Smith?"

Maddison swallowed hard, fighting back the tears. "Err, yeah. Right."

Maddison noticed a pleading look in Chloe's eyes that she'd never seen before. The only looks Chloe gave were that of hate, anger, snobbery and dislike. Maybe the girl had the tiniest bit of compassion after all.

The crowds disappeared, moving along to their next classes. Ben bounced his ball away, stroking his crew cut in disbelief.

"Come on, sis!" he yelled behind. "You may catch something nasty hanging around her!"

"I know you're hiding something, Smith." Chloe came closer, her perfect pixie nose almost touching Maddy's. "And I will find out. Today, tomorrow, I always find out."

She backed away, and there, once more, was the bitter face Maddison was used to seeing. Chloe sauntered lazily down the corridor. "Watch your back."

"Oh, I am." Maddison huffed. "But you are the least of my worries."

Chapter Eleven

"I spy with my little eye, something beginning with…W"

"Wall?" Zakk said nonchalantly, as they had already done darkness, tunnel, sewer, mould, Zakk's foot, Zakk's arm, Mouse's nose… "Kiera, I think we've exhausted all our options now," he hinted.

"This game is tiresome," Mouse agreed.

Silence fell. Zakk and Mouse seemed to welcome it.

"I may just die of boredom." Kiera puffed out her cheeks. "That is if the cold doesn't get me first."

"Poor you!" Mouse snapped.

"How long till the next shift? It must have been two hours by now surely?" Kiera got up and stretched her aching body in all directions. "Seriously, I thought rigor mortis had set in." Beaming a cheeky smile at Zakk, which he returned.

"Trust you. You and your strange little ways."

Alex's head popped up out of a tunnel entrance.

"Pssst, guys…everyone okay?" She didn't wait for a reaction. "Right then, on your feet, troops. Follow me, quietly." With that, she disappeared again.

"She's very flighty, isn't she? Is she always like that?" Zakk asked.

Always." Mouse nodded.

"Well, I like it!" he said.

"Shhh! God, why don't you just wave your arms about and shout 'come and get us.' Let's go," Mouse barked.

"Another hole to go down…really?" Kiera questioned. "I'm starting to feel like Alice in flipping Wonderland."

Zakk gave her a firm shove into the hole.

"Oowww," gasped Kiera, as she crash-landed onto her bottom. "I'm gonna feel that tomorrow." Zakk tumbled out quite gracefully behind as she scrambled to give him room.

"On your feet, guys," Alex ordered, inspecting them briefly for signs of injury. "Are you ready for this?"

Mouse and Zakk nodded. Kiera did the opposite.

"Thought you were supposed to be something special, love."

"I think I've just been lucky so far."

"Well, Miss Lucky, let's hope you are today." Alex almost smiled.

"What's next, Alex?" Zakk's face flushed a little on making eye contact with the elven-featured leader. Kiera could have sworn that Alex took a little dry gulp before speaking.

"Well, the first three you rescue know you are coming and will find you. Take them and proceed as discussed. I have to go before I am missed." Alex turned to leave… "Oh…and good luck."

She seemed to linger on Zakk's face a little longer than her words. With that, she dived effortlessly down a different shaft. The three waited patiently. A bell clanged nearby to signal the changing of the guards.

"Let's do this." Zakk's voice deepened, and his expression read 'serious,' as he squeezed Kiera's hand. "Get your slave out of there as soon as they lock onto you. Keep your heads down, and I'll see you both at the top."

"Zakk…I…"

"Go," he ordered, cutting Kiera off, before stepping into the large mine, merging with the passing slaves.

The girls followed without hesitation. Kiera would follow Zakk anywhere, as much as her inner voice told her to retreat. But why was Mouse so ready to lay down her life? She could've broken out at any given moment. Maybe she was just really loyal to the others, Kiera mused, as she mingled into the crowd waiting for someone to grab her arm. The three scurried about, trying to look busy. Almost instantly, all three felt a hand take them and pull them nearer the exit. Zakk arrived at the mineshaft first and helped the rest as they scrambled to get to the top. Everyone made it back to the meeting point.

"Well," Kiera said, eyes darting round at the five faces. "That was easier than I'd expected." The three slaves hugged their rescuers in gratitude.

"Your Highness." One of the slaves bowed. "We are forever in your debt."

The boy could have been no older than Zakk, but unlike Zakk, he was frail and stooped, his eyes, like his two friends, looked sullen and exhausted.

"Please, please, we are all equal here. Please get up." Zakk put out a hand to assist. The boy smiled.

"I am Mark. This here is Gareth, and the little one on the end is Toni." The small girl started to curtsy then stopped and apologised.

"We are what's left of the Nerakian rebellion."

"Huh?" Kiera frowned. "Nerakian?"

"I thought no one survived the Nerakian explosion," Zakk said, looking puzzled.

"All in good time, Your Highness. Actually, Mouse, why not fill his Highness in while you are waiting on the next guard change."

Mouse shot Mark a 'shut-up' stare. Zakk and Kiera looked at Mouse with wonder.

"Yes, yes!" She threw her hands up in dramatic uproar. "I am Nerakian too, big deal."

"We must bid you farewell, Your Highness. You, too, fearless Kiera. Goodbye. We will see you soon."

"Hah!" Kiera laughed at the boy's strange sense of humour. "You Nerakians are hilarious."

"We will rendezvous when our numbers are greater." Mark bowed as he knelt before the stench of the sewer tunnel. "For that, we are counting on you. We will never forget this."

Chapter Twelve

Tom and Maddy walked in silence along the deserted beach. Maddy gnawed on a strand of fiery red hair, something her mum always told her to stop. Daz used to think it was cute, so nowadays she did it all the more. Maybe he was watching her from a better place. This beach had been a second home. She seldom came here since… This place was now full of lost memories, stolen moments, and cheeky glances. Their first date had been here, every date pretty much had been. The smell of the salty sea brought back memories of Daz pretending to stumble into her, making her closer than she'd ever been to a boy. The sound of seagulls reminded her of eating chips, and the birds hovered above anticipating their next steal. The sea lapping against the rocky shore conjured images of Daz teaching her to skim stones across the water. Her stones sank every time. And now, here she was, back at this place full of happy reminders tinged with a painful sting. She was with Kiera's uncle, who seemed like a stranger. Kiera's uncle…not Daz. She tried to think of the right question to ask; then shook her head in frustration.

"I've never seen the beach so peaceful," Tom mumbled. Maddy frowned at this pathetic attempt at conversation.

"Tis a school day remember. I am kinda bunking."

"Don't you worry about that. I cleared it with your head teacher. She wants you back for your next lesson. So, let me get this straight. Zakk said he needed Kiera's help to save her friend, and she just went with him?"

"Yes. I've already told you everything I know."

"I'd be proud, if it wasn't so ridiculously dangerous. What was she thinking? Why can she never wait? Just like her mother..." Trailing off, lost somewhere in his own thoughts.

"Look, are you going to be straight with me? I mean, it works both ways you know," Maddy said, rooting herself to the spot.

"Well now," Tom said, eyebrows high on seeing her resolve. "Where do I begin? Let's see…mmm…" He pushed his glasses up his nose, wrapped his raincoat around himself and started pacing back and forth.

"Well, please, begin somewhere!"

"There are things you don't need to know at this present time."

"Now you sound like a politician." Maddy narrowed her eyes.

"I am Kiera's uncle. Fact. And you must know I love her very much. I've always known Kiera was…is… *special*. I've worried that this time would come but hoped to protect her from it."

"Well, no offence, but who's protecting her now? She could be anywhere. Sorry, I didn't mean to…I didn't mean that." Maddy stuffed more hair into her mouth in order to silence herself.

Tom sat on a bench, looking out to the sea.

"I cannot say much."

"Yes, you said that already. Sorry." Plonking down beside him.

"There are forces at work to help her. I am doing all I can, all I'm allowed to."

"Huh?" Maddy flummoxed. "Are you even human?"

"Yes, of course." Tom chuckled, a bit like a neighing pony.

"Why can't Kiera know anything?"

"One day, Kiera's going to have to make some tough choices. And when that day comes, I want her to have led a normal, happy life here, so she can make measured choices." Tom got to his feet. "Look, I'm going to have to go. I'm late for a …meeting."

"Great, and what do I do in the meantime? I have all these secrets, and I'm totally useless."

"Just keep doing what you're doing—being a good friend. I'll walk you back."

"No, I'm okay. I'll see you soon." She reassured him, as he didn't seem convinced.

Maddy watched as Tom bounded away, raincoat billowing behind him.

Woof, woof, yap, yap.

Maddy jumped in shock. "Terrence, what you doing here boy?"

"I wouldn't ssay you were totally usselesss." Maddy turned in panic.

"Who are you?"

"Get the dog, too," was the last thing Maddy heard as a large hand clamped over her mouth and nose until she could no longer steal a breath.

Chapter Thirteen

The next rescue went without a hitch.

"Six down. Three to go." Kiera's cheeks flushed with exhaustion. "We're doing this. I can't believe we're really doing this."

"You were brilliant down there, Kiera," Zakk said, over-squeezing her shoulders.

"Ahhem-ahem." Mouse cleared her throat.

"Oh, and you, too, of course." Zakk ruffled Mouse's hair, somewhat patronisingly, yet she seemed content with that. "So, Mouse…" Zakk sat down and patted the space next to him. "Tell us about Nerak. What happened? How did you guys escape?"

Mouse's face paled, like someone had tiptoed over her grave.

"It's okay, Mouse, you don't have to tell us if it's too painful."

"But," Kiera interrupted, "we have nearly two hours before we begin again…whatever shall we do?"

Kiera became uncomfortable when Zakk gave her a 'that's enough' face.

"Sorry…didn't mean to sound unsympathetic. It's just that I can't sympathise if I don't know the details." Zakk fake-coughed in objection. "Sorry, Jude, I mean, Mouse. Which do you prefer? Jude or Mouse?" Kiera asked.

"Okay, I give in!" Mouse flung her hands up signalling surrender. "If I tell you, will you promise to be quiet and never bring it up again?"

"I promise." Kiera gestured a crossing of her heart.

"It all happened when I was about five or six, so my picture may be a little hazy."

"So, about seven or eight years ago then?" Kiera butted in.

"Yes, Miss Pushy-Pants. Are you going to let me tell this?"

Kiera's finger shot to her lips, to show continued silence.

"Nerak was a peaceful planet. No hunger, no disease, no wars. Everyone worked in unison, for the good of the whole."

"Sounds like bliss," Zakk whispered.

"Sounds unreal." Kiera shot her finger back up to her lips.

"Well, anyway, I was a happy little girl, my parents loved me. My sister and I would spend hours playing in the out-fields, or in the vast mountains and streams." Mouse's expression hardened; her eyes glazed over. "Then came the day the skies cried crimson. Mother thought our gods were angry at our happiness. Father pushed us all into the barn, where we huddled together and waited. Thunderous clangs boomed above us. Our world shook until my ears hurt. My little sister sobbed. It must have been too much, as she squealed and ran outside. My parents followed, telling me to stay put, no matter what happened. I was alone, terrified. My family never returned. I ventured outside when the chaos stopped. My world looked like piles of ash; embers glowed where mountains once stood. The earth smelled like burning rubber. A hand grabbed me, hurling me into a container with some other kids. And I've been here ever since."

"I'm so sorry, Jude," Kiera said softly. "I should've never asked you to—"

"It's okay," Mouse said, snapping from her trance. "I'm over it."

"We're here now." Zakk put his hand over hers. "You've been very brave. Let us help you now."

Mouse's naturally sad mouth turned a little at the corners at his touch.

"Can I just ask?"

"Go on…" Mouse rolled her eyes at Kiera.

"Where was the explosion? You said before, about the great Nerakian explosion. So…?"

"I think they just call it that. It felt like the world was imploding. The Witch Queen told us she'd blown it up after we'd left; she loved re-telling us that one. Not sure why she took us though. Guess for child labour. She told me I was one of the lucky ones. I never felt very lucky." Mouse looked vulnerable for a second and then shook it off as quickly as it came. "Anyway, Alex sort of became our leader as she was the oldest. Her brother Daz was like our brother, too, until of course, he went missing a few years back. We all miss him terribly."

"What! Daz and Alex are brother and sister?"

He *was* her brother, Kiera thought. They couldn't have known he was dead. Kiera had this perfect memory of him falling into the darkness, free-falling into a fate of never-ending death. Whenever she thought of their encounter with the Witch Queen, all she could see was Daz's disappearing face. The words, 'save my sister' on loop, played over and over in the cogs of her mind, always haunting her. Kiera shuddered, her skin prickling in a cold sweat.

"It's okay." Zakk jumped in as though reading her mind.

"So, you, Alex, and Daz are all Nerakian…like aliens?"

"Kiera!" Zakk gasped.

"Yes, we are aliens, but so are you, I guess," Mouse shrugged. "The good part about being Nerakian is that for some reason, the Witch Queen's essence-stealing power does not work on us. She cannot drain us or make us zombies. She can hurt us though."

"Let's play 'I spy' again," Kiera suggested, trying to change the subject.

"I think we've run out of things to spy." Zakk chuckled.

The three sat quietly in thought for the remaining hour, awaiting the final guard change.

Chapter Fourteen

The Superman theme stopped Tom in mid-bound. Standing with one hand on his shop door handle, he pulled the phone from his pocket. For a moment, he recalled Kiera teasing him, calling him a big nerd for having that particular ringtone.

"Yes, hello." He recognised the number from the school and expected Ms. Watson's soft voice to reply.

"Mr. Matthews? It's Mrs. Jackson." Something in her tone unnerved him.

"Hello, Mrs. Jackson, what can I do for you?"

"You told me in good faith that you would have Maddison Smith back at school at least half an hour ago. It's against school protocol that I even agreed to it. I may be dragged before the board for this."

"She's not back?" Tom glanced at his watch.

"She's not with you?"

"No." Tom gulped. "She's probably still dilly-dallying along the sea front…you know what kids are like. I'm on it, Mrs. Jackson. Give me one hour, and I promise after that you can alert the police."

"This is again against my better judgement, Mr. Matthews."

"Please trust me. Do another sweep of the school, and don't panic yet."

"One hour, Mr. Matthews!" She hung up. Tom stood with the phone to his ear, listening to the nothingness. How could he have been so short-sighted, leaving her there alone?

Terrence bounded down the street toward him, yapping frantically.

"Where've you been, mate?" Terrence growled, darting about Tom's feet wildly. Then he ran a little way down the street, stopped, and ran back again. "You want me to follow you? Have you found Maddison? Okay, you better not be wasting my time. We haven't got long."

Tom and the little terrier raced in the direction of the school. "Slow down, boy!" The tiny tail-less dog ignored him.

* * * *

"Try not to bring any attention to oursselvesss. We are just bin-men taking out the trasssh."

Googe's eyes scanned the school car park as he pulled a cap further down over his abnormalities. The two blank looking guards opened the car boot and wrapped the unconscious girl in a black canvas sack. Maddy groaned a little, and her eyes flickered.

"Come on, bring her thisss way. Hurry up and throw her into the vortex!"

* * * *

Terrence flew at these enemies before they knew what was happening. Tom wasn't far behind. He panted and puffed, realising how out of shape he'd become. He watched as the lizardy low-life cowered and backed into the vortex upon seeing the terrier. Terrence's jaw was wide and angry as it locked onto one of the stumbling guards. The other guard was frantically dragging a body-shaped bag along the ground. Tom didn't hesitate and ran so fast he knocked the guard back through the vortex. He quickly retrieved the bag and pulled it off Maddison.

"Still breathing." He flopped down next to her, exhausted. "Can you hear me? Maddison, it's Tom. Can you hear me?" She nodded still a little dazed. Her eyes widened on hearing the commotion nearby.

"What the…?" she gasped.

The little dog transformed. In the blink of an eye, the tiny terrier's body seemed to blur and judder, as it grew taller and rolled upward—his paws changing into feet and hands, his doggy-wet snout into a Roman nose. His hazel eyes stared wide, but Tom could still see the dog in them. The former dog/man shook out his limbs, whipped round to face his target and ran at it. This new being punched and wrestled Maddy's last abductor to the ground. Maddy's face crumpled into a puzzle before falling back into unconsciousness. Terrence held the enemy in a headlock.

"Now the dog's out of the bag!" Terrence joked, not even a little out of breath.

"Tie him up and bring him to headquarters," Tom instructed.

"Perhaps she didn't see?" The man/dog shrugged.

"Yes, Captain Terrence, she saw it all.

"I just wanted to tell you, Miss Matthews, what an honour it is to finally meet you."

"Can we do this later maybe?" Kiera panted, shoving her shoulder forcefully under the rather round boy's bottom.

"Reach up a little further for me." Zakk stage-whispered at the top of the chute, his arm stretched out to its limit. "That's it, just a little more." The boy's stubby fingers almost touched Zakk's tips.

"I am trying, Your Majesty. I seem to be a little short."

"Kiera, you're going to have to give him an extra push. You can do this," Zakk nodded.

"Are you kidding me?" Kiera puffed the chocolate stowaway hairs off her sweaty forehead.

"No problem," Mouse said from below Kiera, as she fidgeted impatiently. "I'll push you, Kiera, and you push him. On the count of three, one…two…three…"

Mouse's tiny frame could only manage about an inch. Kiera centred herself and took a mental run-up to the corked boy. Thrusting her body into his behind, letting out a guttural roar as she did so.

"Sshhh!!" Zakk and Mouse simultaneously whispered.

"Got you!" Zakk pulled up the last slave.

The boy fell clumsily into him. Kiera, rather exhausted, and sweating in places she didn't know existed, attempted to scurry up the almost vertical chute. Feet slipping like a cartoon cat on ice. She lost her footing, sending her and Mouse back down the chute. Kiera ended up on top of the frail Nerakian, as they flip-flopped like fish out of water. Mouse eventually untangled from Kiera and pulled her to her feet.

"Thank you," Kiera said curtly.

"Welcome," Mouse replied, making no eye contact. "You go back up first, just to make sure you get there." Mouse smirked.

"Very funny." Kiera clambered back up the hole, muttering annoyances as she went.

"Ladies, nice of you to finally join us." Zakk laughed. Kiera tried to wipe the muck off her face with a dirty sleeve. "Let me introduce you to our three free newcomers. This is Daniel, Lily, and of course, you are both familiar with Jamie."

"Hi." The plump, young boy ran at Kiera and squeezed her. Kiera looked at Mouse's small, thin frame and then looked down at Jamie's.

"Jamie was the Witch Queen's taster. Lucky for him, nothing was poisoned." Mouse chuckled.

"Oh, hi again, J-Jamie. You can let go now if you like."

"Oh, sorry, Miss Matthews." Jamie bashfully tripped backward. "It's just that you're my idol. I've always wanted to meet you; maybe hear you sing?" Kiera shot Zakk a quizzical glare.

"I really think now is not the time." Zakk smiled, putting a firm hand on the boy's shoulder.

"And you of course, Your Highness, what an honour to finally meet you." Jamie bowed and Zakk raised an amused brow.

"Right, let's get you all to the sewer entrance."

The three crouched down into position.

"Hold your breath for as long as possible and wait for us at the end. Your friends are already there. Go, go, go!"

"Bye, Miss Matthews," Jamie gushed.

"Bye, Jamie." Kiera waved awkwardly before turning to retrieve her normal clothes.

Alex's head popped up from the hole.

"God, you made me jump!" Kiera gasped.

"Alex, you made it."

"Don't sound so surprised, Mouse. Of course, I did." Alex scanned the group holding her gaze on Zakk. "Good to see you all did."

Kiera frowned, feeling her cheeks burning, hoping they weren't the same colour as the tomato hoodie she was pulling over her head.

"Thank you for helping us." Alex's tone didn't seem grateful, or warm. Kiera couldn't read this girl at all.

"I'm so sorry." She stepped toward the spiky haired leader.

"Sorry, why?" Alex frowned.

"For Daz." Kiera bowed her head in guilt.

"Yes, me too. What an idiot he is," Alex shrugged.

"Err... I bet you miss him terribly."

"Only when my aim is off." Alex looked confused and then a smile crept across her face. "You think he's dead, don't you?"

"He's *not*?" Kiera, dizzy with happiness, flung her arms around the standoffish girl, who seemed quite emotionless. "That's the best news I've heard in...like ever!"

"Okay, okay! Calm down, Miss Joy. Didn't you tell her?" Alex looked to Zakk.

"No, I thought it was best she found out later, with a little more time."

"Why wouldn't you tell..." Kiera froze on Zakk's expression. "You said I could save my friend, that friend being Daz?"

Zakk nodded sombrely.

"Sorry, am I missing something here? I mean, I know he's a pain in the royal butt, but come on!" Alex's hands flew to her hips.

"Daz is the friend...I thought you meant Joe." Kiera gulped, tears formed so sharply, her nostrils burned. Zakk gripped Kiera's hands.

"We don't know where Joe is. We sent scouts out, after the trees took him. There was no sign of him ever being there. I'm so sorry, Kiera. I thought it would put you off the mission if you had to deal with his loss."

"Oh," Kiera mouthed, pulling her hands away from his, stepping into the shadows.

"Okay, we'd better get out of here," Zakk said quietly. "Kiera, Mouse, you two go first. Alex and I will follow."

"No," Alex protested. "I'm staying."

"No, you're not." Zakk crossed his arms, showing he outranked her.

"I'm staying to save my brother."

"He's here?" Kiera gasped.

"Yes, the witch has him hanging like some prized chandelier over the throne room. When she's angry, she blasts him with her powers. She must be getting stronger, as his screams are lot more regular these last few days. So, you see, I have to go back before she over-cooks him. Daz may be a complete nuisance, but he's my nuisance."

Kiera saw that same topaz flicker in the girl's eyes that Daz had, and Alex looked like a frightened teenager just for the smallest moment.

"I'll stay, too, then." Zakk gallantly moved nearer to Alex.

"No. Who will get them all to safety? You must protect them. You must protect Kiera."

"She's right." Mouse nodded.

"No," Kiera yelped, coming out of her 'Joe' coma. "What if I'm not special? What if my part is done? I will get them back to your palace…only I'm not sure of the way."

Kiera screwed her mouth up, feeling a little ridiculous now.

"I will take the Nerakians," Zakk agreed. "But, Alex, if you cannot get him without risking yourself, then don't. Or at least wait."

Zakk stood unnaturally close to Alex. Her face seemed to soften as he spoke.

"I'll see you soon." Alex cleared her throat and smiled a little.

"Okay, drop and go, people." Zakk herded Kiera and Mouse toward the sewer tunnel like sheep to a pen.

"I'll come back for you," Zakk promised.

"Don't." Alex insisted, but with a hint of fear.

Chapter 16

"Where am I?" Maddy rubbed her head, which felt like hundreds of tiny people had used it as a trampoline.

"You're safe now, Maddison. We've got you."

"We?" she propped herself up in the chair and let her eyes focus. "Whoa," she mouthed trying to take in all of the faces in the room. "What the…"

"It's okay," Tom said, bending to her level.

The room was stark and white. There were a few chairs around a table with various maps strewn over it. No windows, though, and the door to her escape was blocked by yet more familiar faces.

"Hello, Maddison," said a woman's soft voice. Maddison's eyes were still blurring in and out of focus. "It's me, Ms. Watson. Please try to relax. Here, have some water. The drugs they gave you will be out of your system soon."

"Err, what drugs? Who would…"

"She doesn't remember. Poor thing." Ms. Watson passed her the water.

"Maybe that's a good thing." Tom smiled. "You can drink that, you know. It's just plain old water. We're the good guys, remember?"

Maddy sniffed the water suspiciously, then took a sip, and downed the rest. Her eyes adjusted from the hazy film covering them, and she took in all the faces staring down at her.

"You!" She squealed in shock. "And you…and you two as well? What the…"

Amongst the motley crew was a rather stoic looking Madame Swift, Piggy Officer Cole, plus a few other faces she'd seen hanging around town. Mr. and Mrs. Wilson, parents of evil spawns Chloe and Ben, lingered in the corner.

"But you hate Kiera, I mean, your twins are always giving her grief."

Mrs. Wilson stepped forward. She was a very attractive woman. You could see where the twins got their good looks from; it wasn't their short balding father.

"I take the blame for their behaviour. We found out about Kiera when the children were all still very young. I turned them against her." Mrs. Wilson actually looked remorseful.

"Why though? How could you do that to them?" Maddy swung her cherry-coloured boots from the chair's footrest and tried to stand. "I feel a little dizzy," she said, and her bottom planted itself back down.

"Try to rest a few more minutes." Tom offered more water.

"I don't want water. I want answers!" Maddy turned back to Mrs. Wilson. "How could you do that to a kid?"

"We knew Kiera would be called upon one day, and we knew the dangers involved. We couldn't risk our children being dragged into it."

"Like me, you mean?" Maddy spat.

"When you're a mother yourself, you will understand." Mrs. Wilson re-joined her doting, silent husband.

"So, you're all in on this? You're all like spies or something?"

"No… And well, yes." Tom neighed his half-horsy laugh. "We are the rebellion, this side of the vortex. Always ready to keep evil out and protect this world."

"Well that didn't help Kiera, Joe, or Daz." Maddy's voice trailed off. Still, just saying his name, tugged at the seams of her heart.

"We're doing all we can. Sometimes fate is faster than us." Tom shook his head.

"Where are we?"

"The basement of my shop."

"I didn't know there was a basement in…" Maddy stopped talking, her eyes widened on seeing the little terrier with its daft tongue hanging out. "You!"

"Maddison, why are you shouting at Terrence?" Ms. Watson tried to usher her back to the chair.

"Don't just sit there, dog. I saw what you did. What you are!"

"I think the drugs have messed with your mind a little, Maddison," Tom said, assisting Ms. Watson trying to get Maddy to sit.

"Don't give me that rubbish!" Maddy shouted, trying to break free of their good intentions. "I saw that dog change into a man! I'm not stupid, you know."

With that, Terrence's body started vibrating and gave off an odd drilling sound. The little ball-sized dog unravelled upward, into a six foot something, sandy haired, rather handsome man.

"See!" Maddy pointed, feeling a mixture of shock and smugness.

"Maddison, this is the First Captain of the King's Royal Guards. Captain Terrence, meet Maddison."

"A pleasure, Miss."

"He's been assigned to watch over Kiera and her friends."

"Oh that's… Oh my God, what's that doing here?"

On seeing the zombie/soldier who tried to take her, tied up in shackles, Maddy stumbled backward into the buxom Madame Swift.

"What's with his eyes? Are you gonna like, torture him and stuff?"

"Err…no. That's not how we do things here," Madame Swift said, gently pushing her forward, releasing her little toe from under Maddison's clumsy boot.

"I need to know everything," Maddy demanded. She was finally going to be a part of this. The scattered faces all looked to Tom for approval.

"Well, then I guess we'll just have to trust you. Kiera certainly does, and now you've seen that Terrence is a shifter... Are you sitting comfortably?"

Maddison's head hurt with all the new information. Pins and needles attacked her limbs from sitting so long.

"...And that is why Kiera is so important. You must never tell anyone outside these walls. Not even Kiera herself. She mustn't know just yet."

"Wowsers—major head message!" Maddison shook her curls in disbelief.

"Of course, we could wipe your memory if you'd rather?" Officer Cole suggested, a little too seriously for Maddy's liking. The zombie/guard's head shot up, eyes still glazed, mouth open. It began to speak. Instead of a man's voice, a shrill, scratchy voice came through.

"Thank you," said the Witch Queen. "That was almost insightful. I should come to one of your pathetic little meetings more often. I could've saved myself a lot of time. Bye now, folks, I'll be sure to give Kiera your love."

With that, the guard's eyes blackened, and his head bowed as he gasped his final breath.

Chapter Seventeen

"Keep running everyone—nearly there!" Zakk shouted at the stragglers behind.

"You said that twenty minutes ago," Kiera panted, coming to a stop, collapsing.

Zakk ran back and whispered in her ear. "Do you want me to carry you?"

"No! I certainly do not! You may want to give little Toni that offer though."
Kiera pointed across to the smallest Nerakian who looked about to puke from exhaustion.

"Right. On it!" Zakk effortlessly picked up the girl, and she cradled into him. "Last one there's a rotten Pixie," he yelled, winking at Kiera as he fled into the trees.

* * * *

"So, this is your home?"

Kiera pushed through the others to take in the wondrous sight. Although Zantar had been stripped of its beauty, the castle, even in darkness seemed to keep an air of magnificence. Unlike the Witch Queen's spindly, gothic palace, which seemed pointy, sharp and cold, this castle reminded Kiera of something really ancient. Like it could be straight out of the King Arthur legends. It was simple yet grand. Understated, but elegant. Kiera felt a sad twinge, that she would never be a part of its history. The feeling of deja vu entered her mind that she'd stood here before, yet she couldn't have. The royal flags were in tatters yet fluttered furiously in the breeze. Kiera could just make out part of a beautiful lilac tree that was once the symbol of hope here in this now monotone land.

"Whoa, like—you are so posh!" Kiera stood agog scanning the monumental view.

"Weird how no-one's tried to claim it," Zakk puzzled.

They walked single file behind Zakk's lead until reaching the great iron doors, which to everyone's surprise, just swung open. Zakk reached for the lights in the hallway.

"Looks like the power's out. We'll just have to find some candles. Probably somewhere in the kitchen area."

"Oh, will there be food, too?" An excited over plump Jamie jiggled from foot to foot. All the Nerakians seemed enthusiastic at the thought of real food. They continued to snake through the vast corridors.

"What's down there?" Kiera asked, coming to a standstill. Looking into a dimly lit, narrow corridor that had a spiral staircase at the end. For some reason, Kiera's feet spun like the hands on a compass, to point the way.

"Oh…that's…that's…" Zakk's voice trailed off as if too painful to continue. "That leads to my parent's old bedroom. Father hasn't used it since my mother… Let's carry on shall we."

Kiera tried to make eye contact with him, but he turned away, heading toward the kitchen once more. Kiera slowed and dropped to the back of the line. As the group moved away, she hovered in the entrance of the enticing corridor that led to so much of Zakk's anguish. She didn't understand why, but she had to take this route, like a man-sized magnet was pulling her. The voices of her comrades becoming fainter as she took a step into the dark place that beckoned.

* * * *

"So…" Zakk turned to Mark, the oldest Nerakian, as the pair searched the kitchen and supply room for candles. "Did you find anything out whilst you were down in that god-awful place? Anything that might help us win this war?"

"We know the witch is using Zantarians to build up her own energy again. She does some sort of mind-meld with them and the victim returns…well, *different*."

"So we've seen." Zakk slammed a cupboard door. "Is she back to full strength yet?"

Mark scratched his patchy, stubbly chin. His sunken, tired eyes shifted, checking they had no eavesdroppers. "She must be close now, the amount of people she's…used." Mark gulped in the darkness.

"Your friends are very quiet."

"They haven't eaten anything substantial for so long." Mark sighed. "We know what's behind the black doors."

"What?" Zakk stopped, holding his breath.

"It's a huge machine She's been using us slaves to mine for crystals for years. The crystals power up the machine."

"What does this machine do exactly?"

"The witch thinks it will blow the vortex wide open, so that Zantar and Earth will merge into one."

"So, she will be ruler of both?"

"She tried it on my planet, but something went wrong—she ended up destroying Nerak, not ruling it. She thinks she has the answer this time though."

"If it works," Zakk said in a hushed voice, "she could do it to all the vortexes and rule the entire Universe."

"I'm guessing that's the plan." Mark reached into a drawer pulling out candles.

"Right, that's it. I'm going back. I can't just hide here. I have to stop this."

"No! No offence, Your Highness, but what are you going to do?" Mark positioned himself between Zakk and the doorway. "Please stop and think about this."

"She could be using this machine as we speak, and I promised Alex I'd go back for her."

"There is nothing I can say to stop you?"

"No. Now please move aside." Zakk passed the panicked looking Nerakian before stopping mid-stride. "Look after Kiera; don't tell her I've gone back."

* * * *

"Zakk!" Kiera burst into the kitchen… "Zakk?" Looking about bewildered. "Where is he?"

Now shouting with urgency at the Nerakians who gorged on the feasts they had secured, Kiera ran from face to stuffing face, looking for the answer, until her eyes met Mark's.

"Kiera, you're shaking! Sit down. Toni, fetch her a drink."

"I don't want a drink—I want Zakk! Where is he? You know don't you!"

Mark fumbled uneasily with a loaf. "He said not to tell."

"Mark, I must find him. There is something very important he must know."

"He went to help Alex…but you didn't hear it from me."

"Right then" Kiera said, ready to follow.

"No!" Mark sprang up, grabbing her arm. "Zakk wants you here with us, safe."

"You let him go out there alone? After he risked his life for all of you? He could be killed!" Kiera felt her cheeks blaze, and her whole body began to shake.

"Please, calm down, Miss!" Mark shouted, as he and the others moved to restrain her.

"You don't understand!"

As they closed in on Kiera, the glass ring that had been dormant for so long flashed its bright light, forcing them all to fly backward.

"I'm sorry!" Kiera shouted to her dazed protectors. "But don't you see? This is a sign, a sign that I need to go to him. Please don't try and stop me again. This is how it's supposed to be. I feel it." The Nerakians stayed on the ground, looking slightly dazed. "Stay together until I... *we* return...where is Mouse? Oh great, another busybody roaming the kingdom. That's all we need. Find her. Keep together, we may need you if...*when* we return. Sorry again!" Kiera backed out of the room and out of the palace. Heart pounding like her feet toward her destiny.

"Are you crazy? I told you to wait." Zakk pulled Alex back into the shadows before she could pounce into certain peril.

"Man, you shouldn't creep up on people like that. I could have mistaken you for a guard and taken your head off."

"Yeah right...of course you could," Zakk teased, catching an awkward blush appearing across her sharp cheekbones.

Zakk smiled to himself. This tough, elfish-looking beauty may have a soft side, and if they made it out of here—well, who knew what might happen?

"So, what now?" Zakk asked, looking into the dimly lit throne room.

"Look up!"

"Oh—oh no."

He couldn't believe his eyes. Above them, just as Alex had described, Daz hung lifeless like a puppet. On further inspection, Zakk noticed the chain holding him to the ceiling was on a simple pulley system that spun onto a wheel, fixed to the wall. Apart from a slight whimper from the boy overhead, it seemed as if they were alone.

"Let's get him down." Alex pounced forward.

"Wait!" Zakk stood firmly in front of her. "Don't you think this is all too...well...a little easy? I mean, no guards, no resistance, and no tricks?"

"I don't care." Alex pushed past him. "He's barely alive, we won't get another chance like this again, okay?"

"Okay, but I have a bad feeling about this."

"Right, you get ready to catch him, and I'll unravel the mechanism."

The throne room was deathly silent, apart from the juddering of the chain every time Alex rotated the wheel. Zakk held out his arms ready to catch the dead weight of the unconscious boy. As Daz's face drew closer, Zakk could see how much he must have suffered at the hands of the Witch Queen.

"A little lower…a little lower. Got him." Zakk whispered in triumph, gently placing him onto his lap.

Alex rushed to his side, letting the rest of the chain unravel rapidly, smashing to the ground. The noise echoed in their ears as she held on tightly to her brother. The large curtain behind the throne drew back slowly.

"Well now, that certainly was *entertaining*." Zakk closed his eyes, shuddering upon hearing the Witch Queen's voice again. "Really Zakky—very stealthy!" She burst into a violent laugh. Googe and the rest of her mindless entourage soon followed suit. Zakk found the evil dictator's glare.

"Whaa?" He gasped from his very gut—next to the witch was someone he had trusted. There she was, smiling in victory on her smug, overly round face. There was little Mouse.

Chapter Nineteen

Kiera slipped through the darkness, through the sewers and the empty soulless caves. Managing to avoid the zombie guards, heart pumping in her throat, but she didn't stop. She knew now she was the one. In the last few hours, answers had found her, and now she had to find Zakk. There was an invisible pull that always led her to him. Passing the mines, weaving through the maze of yet more tunnels. She found herself standing before a slightly ajar door, from which came muffled voices and laughter. Laughter that gave her goose bumps…like when a pack of hyenas seem to laugh when circling their prey. Kiera peered in, trying to keep to the shadows. It was the throne room, the room where only a short time ago, she herself had taken down the Witch Queen. Kiera's eyes first fell on her tall bony frame. The witch looked totally transformed to how Kiera had last left her. She could make out a familiar voice—Alex's.

"How could you do this to me, Mouse? We're like family—what the hell were you thinking?"

Kiera spotted the helpless three, Zakk cradling an unconscious Daz in his lap. She wanted to sob with relief, and then confusion swept within. What had Alex just accused Mouse of? Kiera shifted a little to get a better view. Why was Mouse at the Witch Queen's side? Why was she smirking? What was going on here? Zakk slowly raised his head in Kiera's direction and gave a look saying, 'stay back.' He couldn't possibly see her, but could he sense her like she did him? Wanting to burst in and feel safe in his arms, but she knew she, too, would be taken. Kiera held her breath waiting for the enemy's next move.

"Jude here is my little spy. Aren't you, dear?" The Witch Queen patted Mouse's head.

"Why, Mouse, why?" Alex screamed.

"Tell them, dear." The Witch Queen's eyes narrowed with relish.

"Zakk is mine." Mouse's tone was lifeless and flat. "He and I will be married. We are betrothed."

"What? Err, I don't think so, sweetheart. We only met a while ago," Zakk fumed.

"Yes, you did, didn't you?" The Witch Queen circled the three captives. "But you see, my little brainwashing machine worked wonders on Jude's tiny mind. It only took an hour or two to make her believe that you two had been promised since birth, and that you 'Prince Zakky' are the true love of her fruitless little life. Jude, Mouse, finally snapped when she realised you had feelings for someone else." Her eyes flashed briefly over Alex. "Yes, my newest invention works wonders. Googe! Bring out my latest masterpiece."

Kiera heard what sounded like a small army marching into the room, sticking her nose in the gap to get a more complete view. A little miffed to see Googe standing with just one soldier. Unlike the Witch Queen's other guards, this one had a shiny-cased exterior and weaponry attached to both arms.

"Whaa?" Zakk shook his head. "What is that?"

"This, my dear Zakky, is my new improved warrior. He is a prototype. Soon, when I take over the Earth, there will be hundreds just like it. I call him J1. He works on my voice command alone. Let's give you a demonstration, shall we? J1 activate!"

The witch's new toy lifted its helmet and faced forward. Kiera stuffed both hands over her mouth, attempting to stifle the despair. The soldier's face was Joe's face. Zakk looked over his shoulder at the gap in the door, as Kiera stepped forward, wanting to reach for him. She stopped. She had to be patient, yet her heart felt like it had broken into tiny fragments and was shattering inside every part of her.

"Yes, this one was a little tougher to crack. He needed top voltage over many days. Too much passion in him, poor boy, but we soon put a stop to that. J1," the shrill shrew demanded, "take the prince and the girl for preparation, leave the other one where it is. Googe, you can clean up his remains in the morning."

J1/Joe marched forward, no expression in his usual warm, pale blue eyes. He picked up Zakk and Alex who kicked and struggled, like they were laundry and threw them over his shoulders, disappearing from view. The Witch Queen swished her cloak to follow as her sinewy frame creaked at the hinges, and she froze in mid-stride. Her back still toward Kiera, she quarter-turned her face to stare at the gap in the door. Kiera's heart raced. But then the Witch Queen continued to follow the rest of her clan. The room was empty now. Kiera counted to ten and waited for her pulse to slow again. Her mind frantically whizzing with seeing Joe again—alive. Her plan was to get Daz out, and after that, she didn't have a clue. Tentatively pushing the door, a little wider, checking if the coast was clear. Running to Daz's side, kneeling beside him, she put an ear to his chest. There was a heartbeat.

"I was wondering when you'd come, took your time." Daz's voice barely audible, as his eyes smiled when they flicked over her face and then closed again.

"Can you stand?" Kiera whispered.

"I'll try."

Kiera put his arm around her shoulder and tried to take his weight. After a few attempts, she flopped back down. The ring on her finger shone its golden glow. It warmed her, and she felt invincible. The strength she found before, when fighting for her life, swept through her blood like an angry fever. Kiera stood firm, yanked the barely conscious boy to his feet, closed her eyes, and concentrated.

"Maddy, I need you. Maddy, I need you…"

* * * *

Maddy's head shot up, her expression fixed, staring wildly. Her skin turned almost translucent. Even her freckles seemed to disappear.

"Maddy…Maddy?" Tom waved his hand in front of her face. "What's wrong…what is it?"

"It's Kiera." Maddy spoke the words, not quite understanding them, like she was reading Morse code from a troubled ship. "She…she needs me…she needs me…now!"

Questions fired at her from all directions.

"How could you possibly know that?" boomed Madam Swift.

"Can you hear her? Is she talking to you now?" Officer Cole took out a notepad, poised for more information.

"Sshh!" Maddy waved her arms to silence them.

"Maddy." Tom spoke very slowly.

"Ye-s, T-om," Maddy mocked. "I'm not stupid, guys. I know she needs me. I don't know how, but there's a real strong feeling in my gut. I must go to her. I can see a vision of the school parking lot, like that's where I should go. I must go now."

Maddy hoped they would come too, as she had no clue of what she would be facing. Thankfully, they followed without hesitation.

"We're coming with you." Tom pushed his glasses firmly up his nose. "Like it or not, you're one of us now."

Maddy loved being a part of something—something important. Maybe this time *she* could make a difference, chosen or not.

"So, where are we heading?" Miss Wilson asked, grabbing her designer purse.

"The vortex." Tom answered.

"The vortex?" Maddy gulped, watching her new allies look to each other in sheer panic.

"This is it gang—buckle up!" Tom said, opening the door that led from the cellar up to the shop.

The tension was deafening as Maddy followed behind. With no idea what was about to happen, she gnawed nervously on her hair. Tom stopped in front of her and whispered, "Whatever happens—stay close."

"Now then." Kiera puzzled, looking at the dishevelled lump that was Daz, as he hung chimp-like from her shoulder. "How am I supposed to get you back through the sewers and back to Zakk's Palace?"

"Take us to the vortex," Daz croaked with great effort. "It's closer."

"Okay, that may be so, but I still have to get you out of here, not to mention the claw trees and that massive rocky crevice…there's no way I can drag you across that…"

"Chill…there's a secret entrance outta here…used it when I was a spy. Also, I know a way back to the vortex, and you won't have to carry me. I think I can walk."

"Well, I wish I knew about this secret entrance before! Won't she be guarding it though?"

"No," Daz gasped breathlessly. "She'll be too busy with her new prizes, Zakk and my sister."

She looked at him behind all the cuts and bruises. His good looks could still be found along with a great sadness.

"Hold onto me. I'll get you there…just point the way."

Daz nodded as they escaped the throne room.

* * * *

"This is the front door—you idiot! It's not a secret at all!" Kiera was horrified. Was he trying to get her killed?

"Exactly, and they won't be expecting us to leave by it, trust me." He smiled, the amber flecks blazing in his eyes.

"I see you're still the same old Daz." Kiera smiled, stepping gingerly through the huge doors.

They couldn't tell if it was night or day outside, everything seemed murky and colourless since the Witch Queen had drained Zantar's radiance.

"Which way?" Kiera's gaze settled on the narrow path of deadly trees that had taken Joe and backed away slightly. "I can't go down there—I won't."

"I told you to trust me—come on!" Daz nudged her in the opposite direction. "There's a quicker way. It's not pleasant though."

"It never is. There are no sewers are there?"

"Wait and see." Daz's breath became more laboured. The two stumbled and swayed through the mist like two drunken sailors on a windy deck.

"Whoa!" Kiera yelled as Daz's arm slipped from around her shoulders, and he slumped to the ground. "Daz! Daz! Are you okay? You need to get up! Stay with me!"

Shaking him. He seemed to be slipping out of consciousness.

"I'm really sorry about this," she said, biting her lip, slapping him hard across the face.

"Awww! That really stung! Evil."

"Sorry, but you left for a moment there, and we really need to move."

"Scwaoorrr!"

The two companions stopped in terror as the familiar sound of the Albatron rumbled in the distance. Daz leapt to his feet.

"She's onto us—move!"

Running as fast as Kiera could pull Daz until they came to a large patch of bog land.

"Okay." Kiera sighed in relief. "This looks pretty straight forward."

"It does." Daz leaned into her a little heavier now, panting. "The thing here is, we have to step quickly, as it's kinda like wading through glue. We go too slowly, and it will set like cement. Then we'd just be stuck here...easy prey."

"Still better than the sewer tunnel." Kiera sighed. "But how fast can you walk in your state?"

"You may have to help a little, but it's not a large area. We just need to get to the other side, to the vortex."

Kiera looked across and saw the swirling mass, their doorway to freedom. It didn't seem impossible.

"Scawrr. scaowr." The Albatron's call became louder.

"Let's go." Kiera yanked Daz's arm.

"Wait," he said, pulling back. "Your chances of making it are better without me. Leave me."

"Pack it up, Firth!" Frowning, hands on hips.

"I'm just saying, don't sacrifice yourself for me, again."

Kiera glanced at the glass ring on her finger.

"I've learnt a lot about myself today—trust *me*. We can do this."

She pulled him forcefully into the gooey mass that almost reached their knees. It was like wading through pudding mix—heavy and gloopy, but without the sweet smell.

"Quicker," Kiera yelled, trying to tiptoe through it, pulling her injured friend behind.

They'd almost made it to the bog's edge when the Albatron's shadow swept across their faces.

"Scwaor."

Daz looked up, mouth and eyes wide open.

"No! No! You can't stop."

Kiera looked down at his feet as the paper mâché type substance turned white and hardened around them. She jumped out onto safe ground as the Albatron saw its moment and swooped in to claim its prize. Kiera's ring glowed brightly; temporarily blinding the relentless pursuer, sending it off course. Knocking Daz over with its momentous clumsiness, catapulting him out of his solidifying mould, he landed on top of Kiera.

"Aww!" she squealed.

"Well, this is new!" Daz joked.

"And totally inappropriate." Kiera rolled him off quickly. "Right. That thing will be back any second. On the count of three, get up, and jump into the vortex. One, two, three!" Kiera pulled Daz to his unsteady feet. "Go! Go!" she yelled, tensing, waiting for the bird's next flyby.

Daz was just about to jump through, but instead, he stopped and turned to her.

"You're coming, too, right?"

Kiera smiled but said nothing.

"You can't save him—the Joe you know has gone."

"I'll be right behind you." Kiera lied. "Now go." Giving him an almighty push, and he was gone. Safe.

Slump—slump—slump. Footsteps, slow and heavy, were coming through the bog toward her.

"Scwar!" Overhead, the mighty bird flew after its prey, straight into the vortex.

Kiera gasped. The slumping stopped behind. A cold breath hit the back of her neck.

"Hello, Joe. I was wondering when you'd come for me."

"We've been here a while, Maddy. Doesn't look like anything's going to happen. False alarm maybe?" Tom patted her shoulder and she puffed her cheeks out.

"Okay, people, let's move out; false alarm." Tom began ushering his team out of the school car park. Maddy refused to move.

"Come on, Maddison. We tried. Maybe you just thought you heard Kiera because you wanted to so much."

"No!" Maddy chewed on her hair anxiously, not taking her eyes from the spot where the vortex should have been.

"Okay." Tom continued, "But you understand I can't just leave you here alone after last…"

"Wait!" Maddy shouted, bringing the others to a halt as they started walking back. "Wait! What is that?"

Spitting out the red stringy hair she'd been using as gum and pointing across the car park. A small shadowy figure seemed to spill from a seam in the air, cascading to a saggy heap on the ground. Maddy leaped forward.

"Stop!" Tom shouted. "It could be a trap!"

But his words bounced off her as she ran toward the unknown shadow. Maddy reached the escapee first, who was face down on the ground. Quickly spinning him over, stumbling backward in shock.

"Oh my God, Daz? It's Daz, everyone!" Leaning over him, touching his face. "Daz? Daz!"

"No need to shout." Daz smiled, his eyes just slits. "You still my girl?"

"Always," Maddy mouthed, as he drifted back into a painful sleep.

"We have to get him to the hospital," Tom yelled back at the others.

Everyone suddenly dropped to their knees as the earth below rumbled like a giant's hungry stomach. A ground shuddering *scwoar* pierced the sky above. The Albatron's metal beak ripped through the vortex.

"Hit the decks!" Officer Cole shouted, as the vulture-like vermin flew low over their heads.

Everyone flung themselves down. All except Captain Terrence. He took a great run up, and upon jumping upward, he changed from man to dog to a mammoth sized dragon. Maddy stared in wonderment, clutching her beloved Daz. She imagined this dragon from a mythical fable of some kind. With its scaly inky body, bat-like wings, and webbed feet, she was happy it was on their side. Its eyes shone like hot coals, and its double set of teeth were ready to puncture. The mutation flew gracefully through the sky, colliding head on with the clunky metallic bird. A banshee-like shriek escaped the Albatron's breath. The pair tumbled, clawing and snapping in flight. Terrence pushed his opponent back through the vortex and out of harm's way. No one spoke as they waited for Terrence's return, but he never made it back.

"Right," said Tom, breaking the overlong silence. "Let's get this lad to hospital."

Maddy stared into space, where minutes ago a man turned into a creature the size of a Navy tanker and attacked a large robotic bird.

"Err, guys…what if anyone saw that?"

"Not to worry, Miss," Officer Cole replied, as he helped Madam Swift pick up a rather floppy Daz. "I'll just report it as another government cover-up—if anyone should inform the police."

"So, this is the world I'm in now. I so wanted to be part of it...now I'm not so sure." Maddison shrugged. "What about Terrence? Will he be okay?"

"He's hardly ever lost a fight." Tom winked. "Was Kiera with you, Daz? Daz, can you hear me?" Tom whispered, lifting the limp boy into the back of Madam Swift's orange camper van. "Did you see her?" Daz smiled and nodded, before he passed out.

Chapter Twenty-Two

Kiera turned slowly, fearing the pain she would feel on looking at this new Joe. Their eyes met, her heart melted, and as expected, he didn't seem to register her at all. Her hand involuntarily sprang out to touch his face when two scrambling beasts burst through the vortex. She ducked, Joe stood firm, unflinching and uncaring.

"Oh, Joe, what shall we do?"

The soldier who wore Joe's face did not respond. Kiera bit down hard on her lip to stop her anguish turning into tears. The battle above continued and the beating of wings blew Kiera around like a feather. Joe stood rooted.

"Time to go," he droned, grabbing her arm. He tossed her over one shoulder and waded effortlessly through the pasty gloop, back to the dark palace.

A ground-shaking thud behind, followed by silence, told her that the battle was over. Kiera wondered who the victor was, and if it even mattered anymore. Slumped across her old friend's back, she had an idea. She believed their friendship was stronger than any magic and hoped to get through to him before he turned her over.

"Joe?" she spoke softly.

"My name is J1. Please be quiet."

"Okay, J1, but can I ask you something first?"

"If you insist." This Joe impostor seemed set on course like a pigeon to a homing beacon.

"Do you remember me, Joe?"

"No."

"Then why are you doing this?"

"Because I hate you."

Kiera's throat tightened, and for a few minutes, she couldn't speak.

"Can I ask why you hate me?"

He said nothing, almost as if he was trying to search for the answer.

"You deserve to die, and my queen will see to it that you do. Now be quiet."

Kiera's mind whirled.

"Joe, do you remember that day last year, when you came first in the two hundred metres? You are an excellent runner—remember?" J1 remained silent. "Anyway, you won, and afterward we stayed until everyone had gone home. You and I attempted the high jump, and the shot put, and the hurdles. I fell and was complete rubbish at it all." Kiera sensed Joe's body tense a little. "Well…I was so rubbish that you'd never laughed so much, and well…I kinda miss your laugh." They'd reached the wrought iron gates of the dark palace. Her plan had failed.

"I don't recall it," J1 said, in a very matter of fact manner.

Kiera let the tightness in her throat go, and tears rolled. For now, she knew, her Joe was gone.

Chapter Twenty-Three

"Welcome back." Daz had opened his eyes and was taking Maddy in.

"Nice to be back," he barked, dryly. Maddy put a straw to his lips and made him drink.

"How do you feel?" She asked.

Daz shoved his head back on the pillow. "Like the inside of a spot." Yes, he looked a complete wreck, but he was *her* wreck.

"Is it too late? For us, I mean. I know I don't deserve your trust again, but if you just give me another chance I…" Maddy planted a firm kiss on his lips.

"Ouch!" He rubbed his cracked lips.

"Oops, sorry."

"No, it's fine." He smiled, pulling her face back to his. "You're worth the pain."

They kissed again, softly this time, and sat gazing at each other until Maddy's face matched her hair colour.

"So, erm, Kiera said you fell? I don't understand how you survived."

"No, neither do I, but I ain't complaining. I think it's all about the timing of Zakk's change. I was falling, and all I could see was darkness and your face. The next thing I knew, I was chained up, hanging like a chandelier." Daz grimaced.

"What is it? You can tell me," Maddy said, rubbing his arm.

"She used me like a puppet. Tortured me for the sheer thrill of it and relished every second. Thought I was gonna die for sure."

Maddy stroked his floppy black mop. Without all the wax in it, she kind of liked it.

"But you didn't die."

"Only because of Kiera. She came for me; saved me."

"Where is she now? Why didn't she come with you?"

"She went back for the others…she has this misguided notion…what were you doing at the vortex anyway? How did you know to come?"

"Well, it sounds daft, but I got this sort of message from Kiera, like we were linked telepathically. It was intense. I just knew I had to come."

"You shouldn't be putting yourself in danger, Maddy. I couldn't stand it if anything ever…"

"Look!" Maddy stood up. "You lot are all saving worlds and stuff, and I'm sat in math class. I've never felt so completely useless, *ever*!"

Daz chuckled a little.

Wanting to be cross with him but seeing him lying there in a hospital bed so weak, Maddy sat back down and gave him a playful grimace instead.

"Anyway, I didn't go off all gung-ho to the vortex alone. I had backup." A smug smile played on her face. "Yes, I have a team now. I'm one of them."

"What team?" Daz tried to sit up.

"Lay down, you idiot. You need time to heal."

"No worries, us Nerakians heal fast."

"You…who?"

"Never mind that now. What is this team, Maddy?"

"I've learned so much, and there's some top-secret stuff about Kiera…"

Tom stuck his head round the door, right on cue.

"Hello, Daz, glad to see you looking a little more—alive."

"Oh hi, Tom."

"Maddison, we need to get back to the vortex. There are some unusual readings we're picking up," Tom said.

"What? You!" Daz sprang up like he had no injuries. "You are one of this team?"

"Afraid so, kid." Tom smiled, pushing the glasses up his overly long nose.

"Wait for me!" Daz threw the covers off. "Just give me a minute to dress. I know I'm sexy, but not sure even I can pull off the whole hospital gown look."

"Daz, you need to rest. Lay down." Maddy eyeballed him.

"Nope, whatever's going down, I'm in. Just give me a few minutes to stand."

"So where is everyone?" Maddy asked, sheepishly, scanning the empty school's parking lot.

"At home I reckon. It is Sunday, babe." Daz flinched, holding his side.

"Don't be clever, *babe*. Where is your—*our* team, Tom?" Maddy crossed her arms with self-importance.

"They're on their way. Daz, maybe you should sit this one out?" Tom said, nervously looking at the boy who was trying to keep up a shambled pretence of being totally fine.

"I told you. I'm here to help—fight, if need be. That evil witch bag has my sister, and now she has my girl's best friend. Plus, it's payback. No one chains Daz Firth up and gets away with it!"

Maddy felt proud, gushing openly at her brave boyfriend.

Suddenly, a bright orange camper van, followed by a police car and a Porsche, screeched into the car park. Car doors banged as Madam Swift's porky foot stepped out from the van. Mr. and Mrs. Wilson shuffled from their silver sports car, and Officer Cole helped Ms. Watson and two other townspeople out of his vehicle.

"Way to make an entrance, guys," Maddy teased. "What, no police sirens?"

Officer Cole snorted.

"Okay, folks, unload the van." Tom looked at Maddy and grinned. "Wait until you see what we have to offer."

Madam Swift pulled open the back doors to the camper van. She and Tom got in and emerged, pulling a huge metallic box.

"What is it?" Maddy asked.

Tom excitedly pulled the lid off and everyone stuck their heads in.

"Whoa, what is all this stuff?" Maddy picked up a large golden sword.

"This is our weaponry, and that, young lady, is not for you, yet." Tom took the sword carefully from Maddy.

"What's so important about that one?"

"This was found in the king's castle, many years ago. It holds great magical powers."

"Can I just have a little go?" Maddy smiled.

"Mmm, a little go." Tom handed it back slowly, and Maddy heard him gulp. "The person wielding it can ask for any weapon they desire."

"Wow, cool!" Maddy waved the golden sword around her head and Daz ducked.

"Careful!"

"Whoops, sorry," Maddy giggled. "Err, let's see, bow and arrow please."

Maddy was astounded when the golden bow and arrow appeared in her hands. She aimlessly tried to master the weapon, resulting in a cracked windscreen on the orange camper van.

"Take it off her, before she kills someone!" Madam Swift boomed.

"Ah, but I only just got going. Sorry about the van." Maddy grimaced, rushing back to Daz's side.

"That's my girl. Don't worry, I'll train you," he whispered, giving a cheeky wink.

Maddy wondered what else he'd been hiding and was looking forward to finding out. She looked across at the others, who were pulling out more strange and wonderful weapons. There were small, round, purple coloured bombs, tiny see-through bombs, oversized hooks, lances, daggers, and swords of various widths and lengths.

"If the readings are correct," Tom said, pulling out a rather odd-looking compass without hands. "There is a lot of movement behind the vortex. Something is happening today—something big."

Chapter Twenty-Five

"Well, well, well, a gift, for little old me. And it's not even my birthday. How very thoughtful indeed." The Witch Queen's insipid tone sent waves of anguish into Kiera's gut.

"Don't do this, Joe," she whispered into his ear. "Try to remember—*us*."

J1 slammed her down. She winced when her left side hit the cold floor of the throne room. The Witch Queen's skeletal frame towered over her.

"Nooo!" A familiar voice shouted.

It was him, her Zakk. Just being near him again brought the tiniest trickle of hope into her heart. Zakk and Alex were chained up in the corner behind the huge gaping hole in the floor that nearly swallowed her and Daz up a few months before. She gulped at the memory. However, could she bypass these fears and face them? Another hurdle to leap. Looking down at her ring for guidance, yet this time there was no glowing, or humming.

"Don't you see, you silly, tiresome girl? I could have had you anytime I wanted—all of you! The sewer tunnels, the royal palace, hiding in doorways…" Stone dead eyes narrowed on Kiera.

"Then why didn't you?" Zakk yelled red-faced, unsuccessfully trying to scramble free of the binds.

"Because you were all so entertaining, and while I was, let's say, a little off my game, I had my little Mousey filling me in on all the juicy titbits."

"So, this was all for nothing?" Zakk barked.

Alex stood quietly, mortified by his side.

"Everything you've done, every sewer you've sludged through, and every decision you've made is because I let you!"

Kiera looked to Joe, wanting desperately for him to wake from his spell.

"Oh, did you think he would see you, and all that effort I put into brainwashing him would simply fall away? Silly little fool." She spat, almost choking on the hilarity of it all. "You see, my dear, you are just too predictable. I knew you'd come back for your little lost limpet. You beat me once, right? Well that will never happen again! And, of course, if you failed to save J1, you would always come back for your brother."

"What?" Zakk gasped, gaze firmly on Kiera.

"Yes, you royal imbecile. Don't you even recognise your own flesh and blood?"

"Zakk, I wanted to tell you, but not like this. I only just found out myself. It all makes sense now."

"Silence her!"

J1 picked Kiera up and wrapped a metal-gloved hand over her mouth.

"So, we are family. What's that to you?" Zakk snapped.

"Oh, it's the answer I've been searching for, my brave, little Zakky. You see, my machine was going to be tested with just you as the key, but now I have the answer. To blow the vortex apart, you and your little sister are like Ying and Yang—opposite ends of a battery. A battery that when heated with the crystals we've been digging for all these years should create a chemical reaction. If I'm right, a nuclear explosion."

"You're crazy!" Zakk wrestled and thrashed about, the chains clanking wildly.

"Yes, I am!" Her eyes blazed with malevolent madness. "Google!"

"Yesss, Majesssty." The loathsome lizard scurried into view.

"Is the machine in place?"

"Yesss, it'sss at the vortex asss we sspeak. We are just waiting on your insstructionsss."

"Good—good. Bring the girl and the prince."

"What sshall I do with the Nerakian traitor, Your Highnesss?"

"Well, let's see. I am missing my special ornament, hang her up where her brother was."

Alex's eyes widened. This was the first time Kiera had seen actual fear from the elfish-looking leader, the girl that Kiera had promised to save. Yet now Kiera was being pulled away by her best friend. Zakk was dragged alongside by two of the dead-eyed guards. They left the palace doors, Zakk put his hand out for hers and didn't let go.

Chapter Twenty-Six

The team froze on hearing a loud growling.

"Terrence?" Maddy whispered to Tom.

He shook his head, the expression in his eyes read terror. They turned slowly as the growling became louder. There, in the mouth of the vortex, stood two of the Witch Queen's most terrifying beasts—the D'rogs. Maddy's stomach flipped, and her pulse pumped inside her ears.

"Don't make eye-contact with them. It's a sign of attack," Tom informed everyone.

With that, Maddy couldn't help herself and looked directly at one. The beast started rearing up, its huge black, wolf-like shoulders angled to pounce.

"What did you do?" Daz turned to Maddy.

"I couldn't help it."

"Defensive position, people," Tom commanded, whilst everyone grabbed a weapon and stood in a line.

Maddy grabbed anything she could, whilst Daz took a lance and stood firm, confident like a warrior.

"Watch out!" Tom bellowed as the first D'rog leapt at Maddy.

Daz pushed her away, pointed his lance upward and into the huge beast. The lance pierced its thick black coat, straight into its stomach. Bile and putrid blood sprayed all over Daz. The beast's tree-like legs gave way, crushing Daz underneath its body.

"Help me move it," Tom yelled at his faithful team.

"Hurry! Hurry!" Maddison screamed. "He can't breathe."

Everyone rushed to Daz's aide just as the second D'rog decided to make its move. It charged at them, knocking and tossing them like skittles, before circling back around for another attempt. As it did so, its fangs bit down into one of the unfortunate townspeople. Dragging him along the floor like an empty sack. Ms. Watson quickly got up and grabbed a handful of the see-through bombs and threw them continuously at the vile black hunter, forcing it to let go of its human meal.

Tom yelled at the others to carry on pushing the first beast off Daz. He grabbed the magic weapon and asked for a harpoon. He aimed it at the second animal, made sure he had a perfect shot, and took it. He hit the beast, right in the neck, and it crumpled like charcoal. The others heaved one last heave, and there was Daz lying flat and unmoving. Maddy dropped to the ground, shaking him rapidly.

"Daz! No, not when I've just got you back…wake up!"

"Man, that thing really reeked," Daz spluttered.

"It's back to the hospital for you, me laddo," Tom said, checking him over.

"Ah man, no more hospital food." Daz groaned.

"You can go back with John, Officer Cole. That D'rog left an open wound in your leg," Tom winced.

"Shark attack." Officer Cole nodded at Tom. "Nothing else could leave such a huge bite mark."

"I'll go when I know this is over. Those D'rogs were sent for a reason. I want to be here when the next thing comes through." Daz squeezed Maddy's hand. "And I'm not going anywhere until I know my girl is safe."

Tom nodded, unhappy at his decision. Everyone looked to the vortex, anticipating what was to follow.

Chapter Twenty-Seven

"Don't do this, Joe! You'll regret this…please try to remember who you are!" Kiera begged pathetically as the Joe impostor placed her onto a plinth on top of the odd metal structure.

A glass tube shot upward from beneath her feet, encasing her inside. She looked across as Googe did the same to Zakk only a few metres away. It felt like miles.

"Two sscrambling ratsss in tessst tubesss." Googe hissed a half-laugh.

Kiera stopped struggling, realising it was taking up all the remaining air.

"Sso, the great Kiera Matthewsss isss now jusst a weak experimental sspecimen for our great Queen." Googe pressed his face up to Kiera's glass tube.

"You'll get yours," Kiera whispered.

But would he? She couldn't do anything to help now. In fact, she'd made things a whole lot worse by coming back.

"I'm sorry," she said, looking across to Zakk, pressing her hands and forehead on the container. "I'm so sorry."

"How touching, you two have found each other at last. And now you will die together." The Witch Queen swished her heavy cloak.

Zakk banged his fists angrily on the glass tube. His green eyes splashed with fire as he shouted hot threats into the air.

"Oh really, young man? Amusing as you are, I've grown quite tired of you now." The witch drew up her tawny finger, pointed it at Zakk and blasted the glass cylinder.

Zakk wailed in agony, as the glass turned orange, slowly cooking him alive.

Kiera thrashed about her prison, trying desperately to smash it. The Witch Queen's wrath hit Zakk again and again.

"Stop it—stop it!" Mouse appeared from nowhere, like she always did, flung herself across the mighty machine and placed herself in front of Zakk's boiling tube.

"And what, little Mouse, do you think you are doing?"

"Saving the man I love!"

"Oh, my poor girl, we really did mess you up good. He doesn't love you; he probably doesn't even like you. I let you believe he did, and the power of love, it seems, is greater than any magic."

"I don't believe you," Mouse whispered angrily.

"Now get out of the way! You're spoiling my fun."

Mouse took a step to the side. The Witch Queen sent another shot of her unmatched power Zakk's way, sending him cascading down into a heap of devastation. A look of horror spread over Mouse's overly round face.

"Noooo!" she squealed, jumping once more in front of Zakk's tube.

Her eyes widened as the blast meant for her prince, caught the child-like Nerakian head on, straight in the heart. Zakk looked on in disbelief—reaching out for her. The petite girl slid down his tube and slumped to the ground.

"What have you done?"

"Put the girl out of her misery it seems. I have no intention of killing you before I've made use of you. Silly girl—oh well." She shrugged. "Googe, turn the machine on. Let's drain these batteries of their energy and crack this thing wide open!"

"Yesss! Oh yesss, oh great powerful Majesssty." Googe leapt forward.

Something strange caught Kiera's eye—a small object running at them and barking.

"Terrence!" she yelled in happy confusion.

The little terrier flew at Googe's wide torso. The lizardy imp ran in circles as if angry bees were chasing him.

"Googe! Control yourself! Destroy the damn creature now!"

Googe continued to flap his stumpy arms and ran off into the distance with a new Terrence-style necklace hanging around his neck.

"J1!" The Witch Queen's nostrils fluttered. "Press the button." J1 marched forward to the machine.

"No, Joe! Don't! You'll never forgive yourself!" Kiera panted, gasping for breath.

"Don't do it, man," Zakk shouted, his voice muffled by the surrounding glass. "Remember who you are! Remember Kiera!"

Joe's eyes flickered a little as he pushed the button. As the crystals glowed, too bright to directly look at, the machine made a whirring sound. Kiera and Zakk wailed in unison as the brother and sister were slowly stripped of their energy. Kiera screamed to Joe over and over, but the soldier looked unmoved.

"I can feel it! My ultimate power shall soon reign over all. I will rule the entire universe, and it all begins here!" The Witch Queen strode back and forth along the vortex, almost skipping in anticipation. "In a few minutes, all I'll have to do is reach out and take it all."

There was an odd mixture of shouting and yelping in the distance. Kiera pressed her face to the glass straining to see the commotion. The zombie guards circled them on the outskirts, making sure no one could get in or out. She could make out figures in the distance, charging at these creatures. It was the Nerakians! They had come to help at last. Kiera watched closely, but it was hard to tell if such a small team of good could be any use against such fighting machines. The Witch Queen had also spotted the intrusion but didn't seem worried.

"Turn the volume up, J1. Let's do this now!"

Joe turned back to Kiera, and their gaze met.

"Joe!" Kiera squealed his name. "Remember me, remember us…you're my best—"

With that, she felt herself falling as her body anchored down the tube. Closing her eyes, her last thought was, *"Joe, I love you."*

Zakk and Kiera slid down their glass coffins. J1 put his hand out to the button and then froze.

"What are you waiting for, J1? Do it now!" The Witch Queen's voice became demonic as she hovered over the vortex waiting to make a grand entrance.

Kiera's eyes fought to stay open. Watching as Joe ripped the button from the machine and then stormed forward, smashing her tube in with his fists of borrowed strength. He tore her from its clutches.

"Thank God," Kiera gasped. "Get Zakk out."

"No!" The Witch Queen shrieked, closing the gap, knees cracking, teeth gritted.

Joe freed Zakk and the crystals changed to a cool white. The mighty machine chugged and grinded. It began to rumble under foot.

"It's gonna blow," Zakk yelled. "Jump!"

The three dove off the machine which combusted into splintering metal, bouncing off trees, showering down millions of tiny knife-like raindrops. As the force hit the vortex, the blast was almost nuclear. A sonic boom ricocheted around the sky. With a flash, everything went white.

Chapter Twenty-Eight

Kiera opened her eyes to view the colourless sky above. Everything seemed hazy. Her brain felt like a sponge, like it was too big for her head. Her body ached and was angry with her. Then she remembered. She rolled carefully onto her knees to stand up. Looking out across this once breath-taking land, it looked like a holocaust had hit it, leaving it a stranger to its former self. Shards of silver still sprayed slowly from the menacing clouds above. A recipe of metal, guards, rubble, and the odd Nerakian lay dotted about the scene. Kiera scanned for a familiar face. Joe or Zakk had to be somewhere. A few yards away, she spotted a mass of blond curls sticking out of a pile of rock and ash. Staggering toward it with the little energy she had left.

"Zakk?" Falling to her knees, quickly setting about pushing off the debris from Zakk's injured body. "Zakk!"

She prayed he had made it. Putting an ear to his face, his breath lightly stroked her cheek.

"All right, sis?" Zakk smiled feebly. "Wanna give me a hand up?" It took every inch of remaining energy to pull him up into a sitting position.

"What happened?"

"Your friend Joe saved us—well most of us."

His gaze fell on Mouse's tiny crumpled body. Kiera's breath caught tightly in her throat, and she couldn't seem to look away from the lifeless little blonde.

"She tried to do the right thing in the end," Kiera mumbled. Zakk placed an arm around her shoulders. "I've never seen a dead body before…it's all very…"

"Surreal?" Zakk butted in, trying to steer her away from the gruesome sight.

"We knew her—it's weird." Kiera found it grossly morbid.

"Living here is hard, Kiera, there are things that you should never have to witness."

The sound of rubble sliding, and people's groans snapped Kiera from her shock. Small groups of survivors; patches of movement could be seen. The ex-zombie guards, somehow broken from their trances, looked about bemused.

"Your Highness," one of them shouted to Zakk. "What happened? Where are we?"

"It's good to have you back, men," Zakk called back.

"So, her power over the soldiers has gone? What does this mean? Is she—dead?" Kiera asked in false hope.

"I'm not sure...maybe."

Terrence ran at them barking wildly, trying to guide them to the whirling mass of the vortex.

"Come on." Zakk slowly rose to his feet. "I think he's trying to tell us something."

Both followed the fearless little terrier.

"Something's wrong, the vortex seems to be shrinking!"

The vortex that was once the size of a small hotel, was disappearing before their eyes. Zakk attempted to shove his hand through it, but it hit solid wall.

"Oh no! Instead of blasting it open, she's sealed it forever." Zakk pushed both hands frantically through his tussled locks.

"I'm stuck here?" Kiera gasped. "I can't be! You're wrong!" Putting one eye to the closing, now coin-sized hole. "I see Joe!" she shouted in relief. "He must have been thrown through in the blast. "Maddy and Daz are there too, and…my uncle?"

"Where is the witch's body? Find it!" Zakk commanded his troops. The soldiers began to move large rocks away in search of their evil captor.

"Oh no, Zakk! Nooo!" Kiera cried.

"What is it?"

"She's on the other side. She's in my world! She's changing—her body's getting smaller—her face is…is…she's changing forms."

Kiera squinted, holding in her breath witnessing the Witch Queen's empty black eyes changing to sparkling autumn almonds. Her jagged black crop grew down her back into silky chocolate curtains that fell around her tiny shoulders. Her dark cloak and dress merged into a red hoodie and jeans combo. Lastly, her high pointed boots turned into sneakers—Kiera's sneakers!

"She's me! She's changed into me!"

Kiera pushed her eye harder against the now, pea-sized hole, watching desperately. The last image she saw was of the Witch Queen/evil Kiera swooping down and putting her arms around Joe. Then, as if she had sensed Kiera watching, she looked up and winked at the disappearing hole in the Earth's sky.

"No! No! No!" Kiera wailed in devastation, smashing her fists against the invisible wall. Zakk grabbed her, pulling her to him.

"Stop, Kiera…stop."

Kiera sobbed uncontrollably.

"Stop," Zakk whispered, kissing the top of her head.

"What are we going to do now? She has my friends. She has my face."

To be continued…

Kristy Brown lives in England with her husband and two sons. She trained as an actress and has a degree in Contemporary Arts. After her first child was born, she began writing a short story whilst he took a nap. That was the beginning of the "Kiera's Quest" teen fantasy series, which is published in e-book form by 'Muse It Up Publishing.'

Kristy then went on to write "Summer's End," and "Summer's Lost," the first two books in her Young Adult Paranormal romance series, which is also published with 'Muse It Up Publishing.' Kristy is currently writing book three, "Summer's Time."

"Just Sam," is a YA/ Teen contemporary romance book, set loosely in the world of tennis. "Cinderfella," is a YA/New Adult retelling of the classic fairy-tale. All titles are available through Amazon in all formats.

Contact: Kristy Brown Author. (Facebook)

Twitter: @KBrownauthor

Instagram: Kristy Brown author

With special thanks to Darrell, Tom, Lea, and my mum and dad. Also, to all the friends, family and readers who believed. xxx

Printed in Great Britain
by Amazon